P9-DYZ-695

SECRETS OF
WAYFARERS INN

Stolen Goodbyes

BETH ADAMS

New York

Secrets of Wayfarers Inn is a trademark of Guideposts.

Published by Guideposts Books & Inspirational Media
110 William Street
New York, NY 10038
Guideposts.org

Copyright © 2019 by Guideposts. All rights reserved.

This book, or parts thereof, may not be reproduced, stored in a retrieval system, or transmitted in any form or by any means, electronic, mechanical, photocopying, recording, or otherwise, without the written permission of the publisher.

This is a work of fiction. Marietta, Ohio, actually exists, and some characters may be based on actual residents whose identities have been fictionalized to protect their privacy. Apart from the actual people, events, and locales that figure into the fiction narrative, all other names, characters, businesses, and events are the creation of the author's imagination or are used fictitiously.

Every attempt has been made to credit the sources of copyrighted material used in this book. If any such acknowledgment has been inadvertently omitted or miscredited, receipt of such information would be appreciated.

Scripture references are from the following sources: *The Holy Bible*, King James Version (KJV). *The Holy Bible, New International Version*. Copyright ©1973, 1978, 1984, 2011 by Biblica, Inc. Used by permission of Zondervan. All rights reserved worldwide. www.zondervan.com

Cover and interior design by Müllerhaus
Cover illustration by Greg Copeland, represented by Deborah Wolfe, LTD.
Typeset by Aptara, Inc.

Printed and bound in the United States of America
10 9 8 7 6 5 4 3 2

SECRETS OF

WAYFARERS INN

Stolen Goodbyes

CHAPTER ONE

The blast of cold air felt heavenly as LuAnn stepped inside the coffeehouse. Outside, the day was hot and muggy, but inside Jeremiah's, it was cool and quiet, and the whole place smelled like rich espresso. LuAnn took a deep inhale and let it out slowly, then moved toward a round table against the big plate-glass windows right by the door, where the summer sunshine poured in.

This was what she needed. A strong cup of coffee and a chat with a good friend. That would pull her out of the funk she had settled into this morning. It had been over a year since her mother's death, and yet LuAnn still missed her every day. Memories would come back to her at the oddest times—the way her mom would have laughed at something on television, or a song that reminded LuAnn of childhood—and her grief would come rolling back.

And it was no surprise that she was feeling particularly tender today. The estate had recently been settled, and LuAnn had finally worked up the courage to start cleaning out the storage unit where she'd stored the things from her mother's apartment in the dark days after the funeral. It needed to be done. She was glad for all the reminders of her mother's life, and she had packed the trunk of her car full of old letters and books. But she was still feeling a bit off-balance, haunted by the memories and waves of emotions that she wasn't quite sure how to process.

Now she pulled her wallet out of her purse, walked toward the counter, and scanned the board over the register. Coffee would help. What sounded good? Something cold, she decided.

"Hi there," the barista said. He had a stud in his chin, and part of a tattoo peeked out from under his sleeve. Some kind of dragon? LuAnn couldn't be sure, but she was pretty sure she had met him before. Micah, she thought his name was. He was a computer science major at a local college, if she was remembering correctly. "What can I get for you?"

"Could I get an iced latte?" Those frothy, frozen, blended concoctions looked good, but they were full of sugar, and she knew the smarter choice would be the simpler drink.

"Coming right up. I'll bring it to your table." Micah indicated the spot where she'd set her purse down.

"Thank you." LuAnn paid for her drink, then turned and looked around the small coffeehouse. She loved the scraped hardwood floors, the exposed brick walls, and the mismatched tables and chairs that gave the place a homey feel. There were only a few other patrons at the moment—a guy typing away on his laptop and a couple of women chatting about their children in the corner. LuAnn recognized one of them as Ruby Meyers, a friend of Janice's from church, though she didn't know the other woman.

LuAnn dropped her wallet into her purse and checked her watch. She was a few minutes early. She decided she had time to run to the restroom before Brad was due to arrive. She ducked down the hallway at the back and went into the bathroom. When she came out a few minutes later, she glanced around the large open room to see if Brad had arrived yet. She didn't see Brad, but—

Who was that? There was a man standing next to her table, and he was—

"Hey!" LuAnn called out. The man yanked his hand out of her purse and immediately started moving toward the door. "Hey! What are you doing?" The other patrons turned to her, but they didn't seem to see what was happening. "Stop!" She moved toward him, but before she could cross the room, he was out the door.

Micah, finally seeming to realize what was going on, raced out from behind the bar and crossed the floor in a few long strides. He yanked open the door and followed the man, who had turned left, headed away from the river. LuAnn followed just behind, but after a few steps, she was out of breath. Micah was much quicker, even in heavy combat boots. She watched as he ran down the block, chasing after the man, threading around the tourists that crowded the sidewalks, but the man was quickly gone from view.

LuAnn wasn't sure what else to do, so she turned around and went back inside the coffeehouse. The women in the corner and the guy at his laptop were all staring at her, eyes wide.

"Did he take anything?" Ruby asked.

"I don't know." LuAnn stepped back to her table. "But I think so."

She had changed out her typical black leather purse for a structured canvas bag with blue canvas handles after Memorial Day. It felt summery and light and, she now realized with a sinking heart, had no zipper and was totally open to anyone who wanted to look or reach in. She saw that her phone was still tucked into an inside pocket, but when she shoved aside her sunglasses, keys, notebook, and various pens, she saw that her wallet was missing. "My wallet is gone."

"Oh no." Ruby's friend was on her feet and by LuAnn's side quickly.

LuAnn felt more and more foolish by the second. Why had she left her purse just sitting there? This was small-town Ohio, and it always felt so safe that she just hadn't thought…But of course there was crime here, just like everywhere else. The mysteries she and her friends had encountered in the past year had proven that. And she'd left the bag unattended right in the front window, where anyone walking by could have seen it. It would only take a second to duck into the coffeehouse and grab the wallet. It could happen so fast no one would even notice. Apparently, no one had. She dug through her purse again, but her wallet seemed to be the only thing that was missing.

"I'm so sorry," Ruby's friend said. "I looked up when he came in, but I didn't really pay attention. I wish I'd watched a bit more carefully."

"It's not your fault," LuAnn said. "I shouldn't have left it sitting there."

"Hopefully Micah will have caught him," Ruby said. The man at the laptop had put in earbuds and was back to typing away.

4

"Let's hope." Still, LuAnn pulled out her phone and unlocked it in case she needed to call the police. A moment later, Micah appeared in the shop window, shaking his head. LuAnn's heart sank.

"I'm sorry," he said as he stepped in. "I thought I was going to catch him, but then he disappeared into the crowd. He must have turned off somewhere. I don't know where he went."

"Thank you for trying," LuAnn said.

"I'm really sorry it happened. This place is usually so safe—"

"I should have known better," LuAnn said with a sigh. She'd traveled all over the world, from Thailand to Rome to Scandinavia to Costa Rica, and she'd never had her wallet stolen. And here she'd basically left the door wide open for the thief.

"You should cancel your credit cards right away," Ruby said.

"Best to call the police first," her friend said.

LuAnn nodded. "I'll start there." She moved toward the door so her phone call wouldn't disturb everyone else, but just as she was about to step outside, Brad appeared in the window.

"What's going on?" he said, entering the shop. The smile that had been on his face a moment before dropped as he looked around.

"I made a silly mistake and left my purse unattended," LuAnn said and explained what had happened. Brad used his phone to call the Marietta police while LuAnn used her phone to find the phone numbers for her bank and credit card companies. It only took a few minutes to cancel the cards, and she was just hanging up when Chief Mayfield strode into the coffeehouse followed by Officer Randy Lewis.

Chief Mayfield looked at LuAnn. "What's this I hear about a wallet going missing?"

LuAnn tried to laugh, but she knew it sounded hollow. She explained what had happened.

Randy got his notebook out. "Can you describe the man?"

"He was pretty tall," LuAnn said.

"With wide shoulders," Ruby added.

"And long legs," Micah called from behind the bar. "He runs really quickly."

"What was he wearing?" Chief Mayfield asked. The police chief was probably in his midfifties, with gray threaded through his dark brown hair. His paunch strained the fabric of his gray police uniform.

"He was wearing a blue shirt," LuAnn said. "And khaki pants."

"What color blue? Light? Dark?"

"Dark," LuAnn said at the same time that Ruby answered, "Light."

"I thought it was more of a grayish color," Micah said. "But he was wearing a hat."

"Yes, he definitely had a hat on," LuAnn said. "A light-colored one. Straw, I think."

"A straw hat?" Randy looked at her skeptically.

"Not like one of those old ones you'd put on a scarecrow. Like a fedora."

"A straw fedora?" The officer didn't look any more convinced.

"That's right," Ruby's friend agreed. "That's exactly what it was."

"They're really trendy," Micah added from behind the counter.

"My brother, Grant, has one," Brad said.

Randy looked around the room, from LuAnn to Brad to Micah to Ruby. Then he shrugged and wrote *straw fedora* on his notepad. "How old was he?" he asked.

"It's hard to say," LuAnn said. "I really only saw him from the back."

"I saw him. I would guess fifties," Ruby said.

"No way," Micah called. "He has to be younger, based on how fast he got away." Micah explained how he had chased the guy and described where he saw him last.

Randy kept writing. "Can you describe the wallet?"

LuAnn told him it was made from black leather, and she gave him the brand and described the silver clasp.

"Anything valuable inside?"

"About forty dollars in cash." She shrugged. "The rest was all replaceable."

Chief Mayfield turned to Micah. "Do you have security cameras in here?"

Micah shook his head. "We don't. But I think the hardware store might." He gestured to the store across the street.

"We'll check with them," Chief Mayfield said. "Is there anything else you can think of? Any way to identify him?"

LuAnn thought for a minute and then shook her head.

"Anyone else?" Everyone, even the guy with the headphones on, shook their heads.

"We'll do the best we can," Chief Mayfield said. "But it's not a lot to go on."

"Best thing to do is cancel the credit cards and report them stolen," Randy said. "That way if someone tries to use one, the credit card company will let you know."

"Already taken care of," LuAnn said.

"Well, in that case, we'll see what we can turn up."

"Thank you," LuAnn said. She knew they didn't have a lot of clues, and she suspected chances were slim that she would see the wallet again, but she tried to remain hopeful. The police promised to be in touch, and then they headed out.

"I'm sorry that happened," Brad said, sinking down into the chair across from LuAnn.

LuAnn shrugged. "Like I said, I should have known better. And hopefully they'll get it back."

Micah appeared with a cup and set it in front of LuAnn. "Here's that iced latte." He gave her a sad smile. It was a good thing she'd already paid for it. "And what can I get you, sir? It's on the house, for the trouble."

Brad ordered a plain iced coffee but insisted on paying, and a moment later he and LuAnn were sitting at the table ready to chat about the reason they had met there in the first place.

"There are just a few details we wanted to run past you before Saturday." LuAnn pulled her notebook out of her bag and set it on the table. "We're working hard to pull it all together, but with such a short time frame we need to make sure we nail everything down quickly."

"Great. I'm anxious to see what you've come up with. Whatever it is, I know Lauren will be pleased."

LuAnn had heard Brad talk about his goddaughter Lauren a few times. She was the daughter of his best friend from childhood, Mark Haywood, who lived outside Cleveland. LuAnn knew Brad took his role as godfather seriously, especially since Lauren's mother had passed away from an aggressive form of breast cancer a few years back. He kept in contact with Lauren and saw her as much as he could, and he'd recently shown off photos of her nursing school graduation. When he'd come to the inn a few weeks back and asked for their help, they hadn't hesitated. Lauren was newly engaged, he'd said, and she wanted to have the wedding quickly, before her fiancé left for basic training. Lauren had scrambled to find a venue that was open at such short notice, and Brad had suggested Wayfarers Inn, the bed and breakfast LuAnn ran with her friends Janice and Tess. They'd agreed to host the reception and had worked hard to pull it together quickly. Since Lauren and her family were two-and-a-half hours away, and because Lauren didn't seem to have strong feelings about the details, Brad was dealing with much of the wedding minutiae.

LuAnn made another note. "Do you have a final count for the guests yet?"

"Not final, but Lauren says it's looking like it will be somewhere around fifty."

"All right." LuAnn looked up. "If she gives you an update, just let us know, but for now, we'll work with that." She flipped to a page of her notebook where she'd sketched out the inn and its grounds. "With that number, I think it would be best to have the tables set up here, under the trees"—she pointed to where she'd sketched out long tables on the lawn under the live oaks—"as long as the weather is nice. It would be a bit cramped inside, but if it rains, we'll make it work."

"I think that sounds beautiful," Brad said. "Lauren will love it."

"We'll keep the linens simple—just white—and we'll use fresh flowers along the tables." They'd work with Tie The Knot, the local wedding shop that rented linens and tables and other party necessities, to get everything set up.

LuAnn took a long pull on the straw in her cup. The coffee was cool and sweet and exactly what she needed. "Do you want to run it past her to make sure?"

"You ladies will make it look beautiful. I trust you."

"Do you think she'd prefer a more formal look? With more structured flowers and real vases? Or do you think she'd want something a little more laid-back? Maybe daisies and black-eyed Susans in mason jars?"

"Lauren isn't fussy, so whatever you think is best."

LuAnn clicked her pen. He'd said that a few times, and though she trusted him, she still had a difficult time believing that Lauren wouldn't be just a bit fussy about the details for her wedding. But Brad had insisted Lauren was busy starting a new job and buying a home and planning for her soon-to-be husband to be gone for months on end, and she didn't have time to worry about decisions like this. She would simply have run off to the courthouse to do the deed if her father hadn't insisted on a real wedding. Lauren had acquiesced, but Brad said Lauren had assured him more than once that she didn't care what kind of tablecloths and flowers were used so long as she ended up married to Ethan at the end of the day. It was a nice sentiment, and LuAnn wanted to believe it was true, but she had yet to meet a bride who truly meant it.

"All right." LuAnn turned the page of her notebook. "Now, the menu. You said you were thinking of starting with an appetizer course, followed by a full dinner."

"If that works for you." Brad shrugged. "If it were up to Lauren, it would be hot dogs and watermelon, but both her father and I think a proper sit-down meal will be best."

LuAnn nodded again, uncertain. She thought a proper wedding dinner was best too, but she wanted to make sure Lauren was happy with the reception. If she wanted something less fussy, shouldn't they listen?

"We can do hot dogs," LuAnn said. "We could even do gourmet hot dogs, with lots of exotic toppings, to make it fun."

Brad sighed and shook his head. "I have no doubt you could," he said slowly. "But..." He picked up his drink and took a long sip. LuAnn waited for him to go on, but he took his time.

"Both Mark and I think this is what her mother would have wanted," he finally said. "When Kelly was sick, I promised her I would take care of Lauren, and Kelly would never have let Lauren get away with hot dogs for her wedding dinner."

Ah. That was it. Brad was planning the wedding because Lauren's mother wasn't here to do it herself, and he wanted to do it the way Kelly would have wanted it done. It was touching, really. As long as Lauren was okay with the results.

"Okay then. I put together some options for preliminary menus." She pulled out some pages she'd printed out. "This one is a little more Mediterranean, with feta puffs and shrimp and hummus as appetizers and fish for the main course. And this one is more all-American." She handed him the second menu, which featured sirloin tips and scalloped potatoes and biscuits.

"Let's go for all-American," Brad said. "Ethan is joining the army after all, and I know he likes hearty food."

LuAnn wrote it down. She was fond of steak and potatoes herself. But still, she hesitated. "Speaking of Ethan...Does he have an opinion about any of this?"

Something flitted across Brad's face. Some look she couldn't read. He lifted his cup and shook it, resettling the ice, and then took a sip. "I'm not really sure."

"Should we ask?" The mother of the bride may not be around to have opinions about this wedding, but would Ethan or his family have thoughts?

"I think it's fine without his input," Brad said. "Mark is the one paying for the wedding after all. We don't need to get Ethan involved."

There it was again. Some emotion she couldn't name passed across his face as he said the name of the groom.

"What do you think of Ethan?" she asked carefully.

"Ethan?" Brad traced his initials in the condensation on the side of his cup. "He's fine."

There it was. Ethan, in Brad's eyes, was not fine.

"What is it?" LuAnn asked gently. "Why don't you like him?"

"I didn't say I didn't like him. He's a nice guy."

"But…?" LuAnn met Brad's eyes and didn't look away until, several seconds later, he looked down.

"But I don't know how Lauren is going to like military life," he finally said.

"It can be a hard life," LuAnn said. "But I suppose she knows what she's getting into."

"No one really knows what they're getting into when they get married," Brad said. "It's…"

LuAnn waited, hoping he would say more. She hadn't heard him say much about his wife, Stephanie, who had passed away four years ago, and hoped he would offer some insight now. But instead, he said, "Ethan is fine. It's just that Lauren is so smart and so special. I thought she might find someone a little more…" He let his voice trail off then said briskly, "Did you know she graduated at the top of her class? In high school and college too? And then she went on to nursing school, and of course she did fantastic there too."

"That's wonderful," LuAnn said. She thought she was beginning to see what was bothering him. "Will she be able to use her degree after they get married?"

"I don't see how, since they'll be moving every few years."

"Nurses are needed everywhere," LuAnn said gently.

Brad continued running his finger along the condensation on the outside of his cup and didn't answer. LuAnn understood a lot from what he didn't say.

"She must see something in him, if she's marrying him," she said.

"He's a good-looking guy." Brad shrugged. "But will that be enough a few years down the line, when he's off fighting some battle, and she's home alone with the kids for months on end?"

LuAnn wasn't sure how to answer. Truthfully, it sounded like a difficult life. But being a soldier was a noble profession, a sacrifice only the bravest, most selfless men and women were willing to make. Besides, no one said Ethan would be in the military forever.

But that wasn't what was really at the root of Brad's unease.

"She could have had anyone, you know?" he said.

LuAnn nodded because she wasn't sure what else to do. "Well, she's chosen him. So let's make sure their wedding is as wonderful as we can make it, okay?" She said it with more enthusiasm than she truly felt.

"Yes," Brad said. "For Lauren, let's make it the most beautiful wedding this town has ever seen."

CHAPTER TWO

LuAnn's phone was blowing up with messages by the time she got home. "I heard about your wallet—did they get much?" asked Emma, who worked at Antoinette's Closet. Wendy Wilson from the quilt shop asked whether she needed anything, and several concerned friends from church called. News traveled fast in a small town, she supposed. She decided she'd deal with the messages later. For now, she unloaded the boxes of her mother's things she'd taken from the storage unit and carried them inside the front door of Wayfarers Inn. She said hello to Robin, a part-time employee who was manning the front desk, and waved to Taylor, who was prepping the café for lunch. She used the elevator to take the boxes up to her room on the fourth floor then went back out into the living room she shared with Janice and Tess. Janice was using a calligraphy pen to hand-letter place cards for the reception using the nearly final list LuAnn had sent earlier.

"How's it going?" LuAnn asked. Janice, a retired home ec teacher, was definitely the crafty one in the group, and she was doing a beautiful job on the cards.

Janice looked up and smiled. "Just fine. I wanted to get a few more done before the café opens. There are some interesting names in this group. Thaddeus Montgomery Beauregard III is my favorite so far."

"Wow," LuAnn said. "Is that all going to fit on a place card?"

"I made it work. How was your morning?"

Instead of answering, LuAnn flopped down on the couch.

"That good, huh?"

"Well, it started with crying on the floor of my mother's storage unit and got worse from there."

"Oh, LuAnn. I'm sorry." Janice set down her pen. "What happened?"

"When I went to meet Brad at Jeremiah's to talk about the wedding, my wallet was stolen."

"Oh no!"

LuAnn filled her in on what had happened, and Janice reiterated the idea that she had to cancel her credit cards immediately.

"I've already taken care of it," LuAnn said. "Aside from a little cash, there was nothing irreplaceable in the wallet. It's just a hassle, on top of the wedding and everything else going on this week. Is Tess back from babysitting yet?"

"Not yet." Janice capped her pen. "She called and said she'd be back later this afternoon. She and Lizzie want to take the kids shopping for summer clothes. I told her we could handle the café today."

"And that big tour group is supposed to check in today, right?"

"That's right." This would be their first time hosting a group from Thatch, a high-end tour company, and LuAnn was thrilled they had chosen to stay at Wayfarers Inn, but if she was honest, she was also nervous. The company had a reputation for high standards, and they expected the best for their clients. The fact that they'd chosen Wayfarers over some of the more well-known luxury hotels in Marietta was exciting, but LuAnn knew they had to deliver if they wanted to see repeat business with the company.

The two of them went down to the kitchen to grab a cup of soup before donning their aprons and serving café customers. Business, as usual, was brisk, and before LuAnn knew it, it was two thirty, and the café was ready for the day's cleanup.

A noise outside drew Janice's attention, and she glanced out the front window. "It looks like the tour group is here."

"In that case, I better help get them checked in," LuAnn said. She took her apron off and took a couple of steps toward the window, where she could see that a small tour bus had just pulled into the lot. "They'll want to get the group settled quickly."

"I'll help too," Janice said. "We can finish this later." She pulled her apron off as they walked to the lobby.

They reached the check-in desk just as a woman pushed open the door to the lobby.

"Hi," she said, looking around as she stepped in. "Wow, they said this place was gorgeous, but it's even better than it looked in pictures." The woman was probably in her early thirties, with shoulder-length dark hair in a fashionable cut, bangs framing her face. "I'm Meaghan," she said. "From Thatch Tours."

"Welcome," LuAnn said, gesturing for her to step inside. "I'm LuAnn Sherrill, and this is Janice Eastman. And that's Robin Rogers over at the check-in desk." Robin waved. Robin was in her early thirties and had beautiful dark eyes and dimples. "It says here you've got ten in your group."

"That's right," Meaghan said. "Eight on the tour, plus me and Alex. He'll be bringing the bags in in a minute."

The eight guests on the tour would use four guest rooms, plus one each for the tour guide and porter, which meant that they had booked all but three of the inn's rooms. "Here is the registration information and IDs for the group." Meghan handed over a packet with the guests' names and information, as well as photocopies of their identification.

"This is great," LuAnn said. "This will make check-in go much more smoothly."

"We like to streamline the process to get the guests settled as quickly as possible," Meghan said.

Just then, the front door opened again and a woman with white hair and big sunglasses stepped inside, trailed a moment later by a man. "This is gorgeous," the woman said, taking in the grand piano and the rock fireplace. "Isn't this gorgeous, Roger?"

The man next to her gave a resigned grunt and followed her inside.

"Over here, Marian, Roger," Meaghan said. "These nice ladies will check you in."

"If that's Marian and Roger Westover, we've got you in Woodbine and Roses," Janice said, consulting the list they'd put together based on the list of preferences Thatch had sent ahead of time. Janice held out a key, and Marian came over and took it.

"Thank you so much," Marian said. "Ooh, look, a little restaurant. Doesn't that smell good, Roger?"

LuAnn had to admit it did smell good. Winnie had made a Thai carrot soup, and it filled the whole inn with a spicy warm scent.

Marian and Roger headed up the staircase just as a young man appeared in the doorway carrying at least four suitcases. LuAnn wasn't sure how he was managing that many bags, but he set them down next to the fireplace, gave a jaunty wave, and headed back out.

"That's Alex," Meaghan said. "He'll need to see the list of room assignments when we're done here so he can deliver the bags to the right rooms."

"Sure thing." To LuAnn's right, Robin was handing a key to a couple in matching polo shirts and khaki shorts. Another couple stepped up to LuAnn.

"Oh my goodness, this place is just beautiful," the woman said. She was probably ten years older than LuAnn, if LuAnn had to guess, and had a lilting Southern accent. "They told us there's an honest-to-goodness tunnel underneath the inn that was used in the Underground Railroad. I can't wait to see it. I just love history. I was a history teacher for years, and I can't believe I'm finally going to get to see something I taught my students about."

She had an open, warm air about her, and LuAnn liked her immediately.

"I was a history teacher too," LuAnn said. "What grade did you teach?"

"Middle school," the woman said. "In Lexington, Kentucky. Though my people are originally from just outside Louisville." She pronounced the name of the city with a series of slurred vowel sounds in the middle, and LuAnn had to smile at the Southern turn of phrase.

"I taught high school history and English in Clarksburg, West Virginia." She smiled at the woman and continued, "Not too far from the small town way up in the West Virginia mountains where *my* people are from. And now I live here. I'm LuAnn Sherrill."

"Jacqueline Carroll," she said, laughing. "Hey, we rhyme."

LuAnn laughed and glanced down at the registration sheet. "That must make you Jay Carroll." She turned to the man standing just a step behind Jacqueline. He stood still, his eyes wide and his mouth open.

"Jay," his wife said, nudging him with an elbow, "this is where you introduce yourself."

Jay didn't move. He was staring at LuAnn.

"Are you okay?" LuAnn said. His skin looked pale, and he hadn't blinked or acknowledged that anyone had spoken to him. It was almost...Well, it was hard to read, but the word that came to LuAnn unbidden was *haunted*.

"Jay?" Jacqueline turned and looked at him now. "Is everything okay? Is it your heart?"

"Yes—I mean no—I mean yes, I'm okay, and no, it's not my heart." Jay shook his head. He blinked and looked away from

LuAnn, and he laughed. Whatever spell had kept him fixated on her had been broken. "I'm fine."

"Thank goodness," Jacqueline said. "I was afraid it was another heart attack for a minute there."

"No, no. I'm fine." A smile spread across his face, but it didn't reach his eyes. His eyes showed some other emotion entirely. "Sorry to scare you. It must be this heat."

"Let's get you upstairs so you can lie down for a bit," Jacqueline said.

"We've got you in Moonlight and Snowflakes," LuAnn said. She took the key out of the drawer and handed it to Jacqueline. "One of my favorite rooms. You'll have a wonderful view of the river."

"Thank you." Jacqueline started to turn toward the stairs.

"You might want to use the elevator," LuAnn said, indicating the door through the café. "The room is on the third floor, and—"

"I'm fine," Jay said. "I can handle the stairs."

"Okay," Jacqueline said. "Just don't you go dying on me. That would sure ruin the trip."

LuAnn wanted to laugh, but just before Jay turned to follow his wife, he cast one last look back at LuAnn, and a shiver ran through her. It was as if he were seeing something deep inside her. It was unnerving, but more than that, it was...it was strange. LuAnn had the oddest sense that she'd met him somewhere before. That she knew him somehow. She searched her memory, trying to unearth any scrap of remembrance. Had she met him before?

"Are you all right?" Janice asked after she'd handed the keys to Lily and Lace to the next couple.

"I'm fine." LuAnn turned back to the desk. Between her, Janice, and Robin, it only took a few minutes to get the rest of the group checked in, and after Alex left to carry bags up to the rooms, Janice turned to LuAnn.

"What's wrong?"

"Nothing." Then, a moment later, "I don't know."

"What do you mean?"

"One of the men who checked in. Jay Carroll. Something about him seemed familiar."

"The man who got spooked when he saw you?"

"That's a good word for it," LuAnn said.

"I definitely noticed him," Janice said. "Because of his hat."

"His hat?" LuAnn frowned. "He wasn't wearing a hat."

"No, he wasn't. He took it off when he came inside. But it was in his hands."

"It was?" LuAnn played back the scene in her mind and realized she hadn't noticed a hat.

"It was. And guess what kind of hat it was?"

LuAnn gestured for Janice to spit it out.

"It was a straw hat. Like a fedora, with a band of blue ribbon around the crown."

LuAnn felt her heartbeat speed up. "Are you sure?"

"I am sure. I thought it was strange, because you'd just finished telling me about how the man who stole your wallet had one."

"Oh, Janice." LuAnn reached to take her arm. "You don't think…"

"I don't know," Janice said. "I didn't see the man at the coffeehouse, and I would hate to think badly of one of our guests."

LuAnn considered. So this man had a hat similar to one worn by the man who had taken her wallet. That was hardly enough to suspect him.

"But he did act strangely when he saw you," Janice said.

LuAnn thought this through. Her wallet had contained her driver's license, which showed her picture and gave her name. If Jay had seen her license, it could explain why he'd acted so strangely. And the only way he would have seen her license was if…

"He was wearing a blue shirt too, wasn't he?" LuAnn thought back to the image of Jay standing frozen in front of her.

"He was. Navy blue," Janice confirmed.

"Still. Navy blue is a very common color," LuAnn said. "And he had a hat. But so do many Southern gentlemen."

"I'm not saying it was him," Janice said. "I'm just pointing out that it seems an odd bit of a coincidence."

"And that it would explain why he seemed so surprised to see me," LuAnn added.

"Exactly." Janice nodded.

"But the guy who took my wallet was younger," LuAnn said. "Jay has to be in his seventies."

"I thought you didn't see him?"

"Not up close, but surely I would have been able to tell the difference between a man in his fifties and a man in his seventies. And the man who took my wallet ran away so quickly. Surely a man in his seventies couldn't run like that."

"I'm just saying don't write it off. It's possible."

"It's only possible if the tour bus got here early, and the group was roaming around downtown. There's no reason for us to think they didn't just arrive in town when they checked in here."

"You're right. But there's only one way to find out whether or not that's true. We would need to do some more investigating to find out for sure."

LuAnn agreed. She had a strong feeling she would be doing just that.

CHAPTER THREE

June 1, 1859

Prudence Willard held her husband's mother close. Hester smelled of talcum and of cinnamon, and Prudence didn't want to let go.

"Take care of thyself now," Hester said, pulling back after a moment. "And take care of that babe." She had tears rimming her eyes. Prudence couldn't look at her, or they would both start crying.

"I will. I will do everything I can to keep him safe."

Hester Willard adjusted the shawl around her shoulders. She hesitated until the driver stepped forward. "We must go, or you will miss the train," he said quietly. The buggy was waiting to take them to the train station. The horses stomped their feet impatiently. The low clouds threatened rain, the sky gray and moody.

"I just want to hug that babe one more time," Hester said. Jason stepped forward and held out the tiny bundle that was Moses, Prudence's long-awaited infant son. Jason's mother had traveled for several days, between two different trains and slow-moving buggies over winding dirt roads, to get here to meet her grandson, and her visit had been too short. Prudence knew that Hester did not want to go. Hester reached out and took her small grandson and held him against her chest. She murmured something Prudence couldn't hear under her breath—Prudence was sure it was a blessing—and finally, with a sigh, she handed her grandson back to Jason. She leaned in and gave her son one last hug and then allowed the driver to help her into the buggy.

"We will write with news," Jason said. Hester nodded, settling her skirts around her, and waved as the carriage started to move. The jostling had awakened little Moses, and he was working himself into an indignant cry. Prudence took her small son from Jason's arms, and as she bounced and rocked him, he settled some. They stood—their little family—in the lane and watched as the buggy carried Jason's mother away. By the time it disappeared from sight, they were all crying.

"She will come again," Prudence said. She turned and headed toward the house. She had to get this little one fed.

Jason turned to follow her. Patience the goose squawked and ran across the drive as they neared.

"Or perhaps we will go see her," Prudence added. "Perhaps next summer. Then thee could see thy brother again, and his family."

Jason nodded. Prudence wasn't sure how this would be possible—they had a farm to run, not to mention her other, covert activities, but it made her hopeful to say it.

"Moses needs to know his grandmother."

Jason didn't say anything, but Prudence was used to that. He was quiet, just as he always had been. He spoke when something needed to be said. He turned and headed out the back door. To the barn, no doubt. There were many chores that had been neglected during the visit, and Jason would no doubt throw himself into the work now to ease the ache.

She settled into a chair and started to nurse the baby. His angry crying stopped as he drank, and his little body relaxed. What she hadn't said, what she didn't need to say, was that Jason's mother was the only blood grandparent Moses had. Anna was… Well, Anna Barton was like family, but when it came down to it, she was not. And Prudence's parents were long gone.

Or at least, she thought, reaching for a cup of water Jason had thoughtfully set nearby, as far as she knew they were. She hadn't heard from her parents in over a decade—not since the day—

But no. She couldn't bring herself to think about the day when obedience to her mother and father meant that she leave them behind as she ran to freedom. Four years earlier the three of them had been captured and enslaved by those who thought it possible to own another human being. She hadn't heard from or seen either of her parents since they'd arranged for her escape. She'd accepted long ago that they were gone. That even if they were alive somewhere, they were no doubt still enslaved and that she'd never be able to find them. She had mourned them and tried to forget.

But now, as she held her tiny son in her arms, as she remembered Hester's face, so filled with love as she gazed down at her grandson, Prudence wondered. If they were out there somewhere—if there was any chance they were still alive—they deserved to know about Moses. They deserved to know that they had a grandson and that he was beautiful. That he had the dark eyes of his grandfather and the light skin that meant he'd never face the same enslavement others had endured. That he was loved and cherished and that he would live free.

But how could she find out for sure if they were gone? How could she really know? She didn't have the slightest idea where to start.

But as she sat there, her tiny son at her breast, a plan began to form.

CHAPTER FOUR

LuAnn was helping Winnie clean up the kitchen when she heard footsteps on the stairs.

"I'll be right back, Winnie," she said, setting down the rag she'd been using to wipe Big Red, their hardworking stove painted a glorious shade of fire engine red. "I should go make sure that's not a guest needing something." Tess was out picking up groceries and Janice was upstairs working on the place cards for the wedding, so LuAnn was keeping an eye on the business of the inn.

"Okay," Winnie said. LuAnn knew Winnie could clean the whole kitchen with her eyes closed, but the three ladies still helped so the burden of running and cleaning the kitchen didn't all fall to her. LuAnn walked out of the kitchen and through the café into the lobby. She found Meaghan, the tour director, looking down at a clipboard.

"Is everything all right?" LuAnn asked.

Meaghan looked up and smiled. "Oh, yes, thank you. Everything is great. The inn is beautiful."

"Thank you. If there's anything you need, please don't hesitate to let us know."

"I appreciate it." Meaghan looked around and let out a soft sigh. "It must be nice to wake up every morning in a place like this."

"It is pretty nice. We feel very blessed," LuAnn admitted. "But what about you? You have just about the coolest job in the world, touring amazing places, staying in nice hotels, eating at the best restaurants. It sounds pretty great."

"I do enjoy it," Meaghan said. "For now, anyway. It's hard to maintain any kind of normal social life when I travel so much. Eventually I'd like to settle down and get married. But for now, it's pretty ideal." She glanced down at her clipboard. "It's just a lot of details to juggle."

"I can imagine." LuAnn knew a few of the people from the tour group had gone for a walk along the river, but most were upstairs resting. "What do you have planned for the rest of the day?"

"We have a private tour of the Campus Martius this evening, just after it closes for the day. And then there's dinner at the Lafayette Hotel after that."

"A private tour? How did you swing that?" The Campus Martius was one of the earliest fortifications in what was then the Northwest Territory, and the beautiful old buildings were now a popular museum showcasing an important piece of Ohio history.

"That's the kind of thing you get on Thatch tours. The company does tours all over the world and is very good at arranging events like after-hours tours. I guess part of what you're paying for on these tours is exclusive access. And hey, I guess if you can afford it, why not?"

"That's wonderful." LuAnn felt grateful, once again, that the inn had been included on the tour. She wanted to make sure they were considered in the future as well. But she also had another goal in mind, since she had Meaghan alone. "And what about the people on the tour? Do you enjoy them? Do you ever have any problems?"

"For the most part, they're pretty great," Meaghan said. "They're here because they're interested in history and travel, and they always have unique life stories they like to share. I mean, of course there's always one or two in every group that can be a challenge, and I guess if you're paying this much for a tour, you can expect them to have high standards. But most of them are nice enough."

"I got a chance to talk with Jacqueline Carroll and her husband when I was checking them in," LuAnn said. "They seemed really lovely."

"Oh yeah, Jacqueline is wonderful. She's friendly and fun to talk to. Jay is quieter, but he seems nice. But we just started the tour yesterday in Amish country, so there's plenty of time."

LuAnn had all kinds of questions about that. Amish country? Where had they stayed? What had the group thought of the simple life? But she needed to focus on her goal. "What do you know about Jay and Jacqueline? Do you know what brought them on the tour?"

"I don't know a ton," Meaghan admitted. "That stuff usually comes out over the course of the tour. All I really know is what was on the information sheet I got at the beginning of the tour. They're from Lexington, Kentucky. And they can clearly afford to pay for this tour, so they must be doing all right. I'm not really sure of much else."

LuAnn nodded. She'd known that already, and none of it suggested any reason for Jay's reaction when she'd checked them in. She wasn't sure how to find out more on that front, so she decided to try a different approach. Janice had suggested that Jay could have been the one to take her wallet, and LuAnn still thought that was a bit farfetched, but she might as well find out whether it was even a possibility.

"I hope you all love Marietta. It's such a pretty little town, and so full of history. Did you get a chance to see any of the sights yet? Or did you all come straight here when you got to town?"

"We got in a little while before it was time to check in, so we had about an hour to walk around and grab lunch before coming here," Meaghan said.

"Did you do that as a group, or with everyone on their own?"

"Everyone did their own thing. I told them to meet me back at the bus at two, and pretty much everyone was on time."

LuAnn tried to find a way to phrase her next question that didn't seem intrusive.

"Do you know what people did during that time?"

Meaghan shrugged. "I think there was a group that went to that great pizza place over on Front Street." That would be Over the Moon Pizza, LuAnn knew. "And I think some went to that sandwich shop near the library. But I'm not really sure."

"Do you have any idea what Jay and Jacqueline did?"

Meaghan gave her a strange look. And, okay, maybe that had crossed the line. "I'm not really sure," she said. "You'd have to ask them." And then, after a pause, "Why?"

LuAnn thought quickly. "Jacqueline mentioned to me that she was a history teacher. So was I. I was going to suggest that she check out the Gallery if she didn't go there today. It's in a beautiful old building I thought she might enjoy."

It was flimsy at best, and Meaghan's wrinkled brow wasn't an encouraging sign. But it was true—the building was right in the heart of town, and it was historic, even if the art gallery inside was not.

"Oh. Well, I'm sure she'd be happy to check it out."

LuAnn decided she'd better get out of there before Meaghan had time to ask any more questions about that. She wanted to leave a good impression so Thatch Tours would come back, not scare them away with her nosy questions.

"Well, if you have any questions, or if there's anything at all you need, please don't hesitate to ask any of us," LuAnn said. "We're so honored that you're here."

"Thank you." Meaghan smiled and turned back to her clipboard. "I really appreciate it."

LuAnn turned and headed back into the kitchen to finish cleaning up. She hadn't figured out why Jay had reacted so strangely at check-in, though she'd just learned from Meaghan that it was theoretically possible that he was the wallet-snatcher. He'd had the opportunity, at any rate. That was still a long way from proving he did it, and LuAnn had her doubts. Still, though. Something was definitely strange about the way he reacted when she'd checked them in. She couldn't put her finger on it, but...

Well, it had almost been like he'd seen a ghost.

CHAPTER FIVE

After the three innkeepers had eaten dinner in their apartment, LuAnn and Tess went downstairs. Tess was going to lock up for the night, and LuAnn had left her notebook in the office. She ducked into the small office and found the notebook, and then she went out to the lobby, where she saw that Tess was sitting on one of the couches, her feet up on the coffee table.

"The tour bus just pulled in," Tess said before LuAnn had a chance to ask. "I figured it made sense to wait until they came in before locking the doors."

"Yes, I suppose it does," LuAnn said and sat down on the couch next to her. "You know, this couch is really not that comfortable."

"No, it's really not," Tess agreed. It was a reproduction of a Louis XVI settee upholstered in deep blues and greens. It had belonged to Janice, and it looked beautiful in the lobby, but LuAnn had never spent much time sitting on it. "It's a good thing we don't often have time to sit."

"I suppose you're right," LuAnn said as the front door opened. Meaghan stepped in first, clipboard in hand. She was followed by a woman LuAnn recognized as Marian Westover, followed by her husband, Roger, and then the rest of the group came in, most of them talking and laughing.

"How was your dinner?" LuAnn asked. She directed the question at no one in particular, but a woman in a beret answered.

"It was wonderful. Best clams I ever ate. And the atmosphere was lovely."

Mona. LuAnn was pretty sure her name was Mona. Mona from Arizona.

"Such a beautiful restaurant," another one added. The group started up the stairs, but LuAnn noticed Jay and Jacqueline hovering at the entrance to the café.

She started to rise, but the couch was really low, and Tess had to help her, laughing, and then LuAnn turned and helped Tess.

"That'll teach us to sit down on the job," Tess said as she walked across the room toward the café. "Can I help you with something?"

Jay and Jacqueline turned, and Jacqueline's face broke into a soft smile. But Jay's face—was LuAnn imagining it? He had looked at her but didn't meet her eye, and he immediately looked away as he spoke. "I was wondering if it was possible to get a glass of milk," he said. "I take a medicine that upsets my stomach, and taking it with milk often helps."

"Of course," LuAnn said. "Do you prefer whole milk? Or skim?"

"Whole, please," Jay answered, his eyes trained on the ground.

"I can't stand that anemic skim stuff," Jacqueline said, laughing. "The more fat the better, I say."

"Coming right up." LuAnn headed through the café toward the kitchen. She heard Tess introduce herself to the couple, but her mind was on something else, something niggling just on the edge of her consciousness. What was it? Something about what Jay said had struck her. She stepped into the dark kitchen and took down a clean glass from the cabinet. She opened the industrial-sized refrigerator and pulled out the gallon jug of whole milk. As she filled the glass she thought back through the exchange. What was it that had bothered her about it?

Tess was still chatting with the couple when LuAnn carried the milk back into the lobby. "Here you are," she said as she handed the glass to Jay.

He took it and thanked her. But then, instead of turning away, he looked directly at her, watching her, for just a bit too long. He wasn't staring at her, exactly, but there was something uncomfortable in his gaze, something a little too direct. LuAnn suddenly felt like he was trying to see all the way into her.

"We sure do appreciate it," Jacqueline said and turned toward the stairs. Jay's gaze broke away from LuAnn, and he followed just a step behind his wife. LuAnn felt unsettled as she watched them climb the first flight of stairs and then continue up to the third floor. Something about this man was off. Why had he avoided looking at her at first? And then stared at her? Was Janice right? Did it have to do with her missing wallet? It was possible, she thought. But LuAnn couldn't help but think it was more than that.

"Did you see that?" LuAnn asked.

"See what?"

"He wouldn't look at me before I went to get the milk, and then he wouldn't stop looking at me."

"I didn't notice." Tess laughed. "Maybe he was just really excited about the milk."

Tess made a joke about everything. That was what she did. And usually LuAnn appreciated the way her humor defused most situations. But something about the way Jay had acted around her was disconcerting, and she wasn't sure it was something to joke about.

"They're nice," Tess continued. "And she's a hoot. A Southern belle, born and bred. I chatted with them while you got the milk. She grew up on a horse farm and went to cotillions and had a debutante ball and everything. And he's from Columbus, from 'the wrong side of the tracks.' She actually used that phrase, which, hello, no one really says that, do they? Anyway, I get the sense that it was a whole forbidden love kind of thing. Which is so sweet."

"You got all that while I went to get the milk?"

Tess shrugged. "I just asked where they're from. I think she would have told me her life story and more if you'd been gone much longer."

LuAnn smiled. Jacqueline was outgoing and entertaining—that was clear just from the few interactions they'd had. But Jay…

LuAnn was still thinking about it when Tess went over and locked the door, and they took the elevator to the fourth floor.

"It sounded like the tour group came back," Janice said. While they were downstairs, she'd finished cleaning up the dinner dishes and was seated at the table working on the place cards again.

"They're all back and up in their rooms for the night," LuAnn said.

"And LuAnn thinks one of them is creepy," Tess said.

"I didn't say he was creepy," LuAnn said. "Just strange."

"That Jay guy?" Janice asked.

LuAnn nodded.

"What happened? Did he say something?"

"It's not what he said." LuAnn shook her head. "It was just that he wouldn't look at me at first, and then he wouldn't look away."

"I didn't notice anything strange," Tess said at the same time that Janice said, "Do you think he did it?"

"Did what?" Tess turned and looked at Janice like she was crazy.

"Took her wallet," Janice said.

Tess tilted her head, confused, and Janice continued to spell out her theory. "When he checked in, he was wearing a blue shirt and a straw hat, just like the guy who took your wallet from the coffeehouse, right?"

"Yes," LuAnn said.

"And you said the tour group had time to wander around town before they checked in," Janice continued. "Which means that he was in the area at the right time."

"We don't know if he was anywhere near the coffeehouse, to be fair," LuAnn said. "Just that the tour group had some free time, and he could possibly have been there."

"So that's something we need to find out to prove it," Janice said. "We can ask him tomorrow where he went. But no matter what he says, it doesn't change the fact that he looked like he'd seen a ghost when he saw LuAnn at the check-in desk. Which would make perfect sense if he'd just stolen her wallet. He clearly didn't expect to see the person he'd just pickpocketed at the inn where he was staying."

Tess looked from Janice to LuAnn and back again. "Are you serious?"

"Totally," Janice said.

LuAnn shrugged, unsure what to say.

"I mean, I guess it's theoretically possible," Tess said as she lowered herself into an armchair. "But your story has a lot of holes in it."

"Like what?"

"First of all, it's all circumstantial," Tess said. "The guy who took the wallet was wearing a hat, and so was Jay?"

"They were also both wearing blue shirts," Janice said.

"Probably half the men in America wear blue shirts on any given day."

"And what about the fact that Jay is probably in his seventies?" LuAnn jumped in. "Did he really sprint away from the scene of the crime?"

Janice was unperturbed. "It's possible."

"Secondly, if he got spooked because he recognized LuAnn from the driver's license in the wallet he'd just stolen, wouldn't he have recognized the address too? So why would he have been surprised when he showed up, and she was here?"

"They're on a group tour," Janice said. "The whole point of one of those is that you don't have to pay attention to things like the address of your hotel. You just get on a bus and go. He might have known the name of the inn, but I would wager that not one person on this tour paid any attention to the address."

LuAnn had to admit Janice had a point there. Now that she'd said it like that, it did seem unlikely that Jay or anyone would have put together the address on her license with Wayfarers Inn.

"And have you seen how much these tours cost?" Tess asked. "If you can afford to go on this tour, you're not stealing wallets for pocket change."

"The tour is expensive. All the more reason to need money," Janice said. "Besides, you didn't see it. The way he looked at LuAnn this afternoon...Something was definitely up. Like I said, it was like he'd seen a ghost. His skin got pale, and he literally took a step back."

"He's on medication," Tess said. "Maybe there was a medical reason for that."

"Maybe," Janice said. "But maybe there's a more immediate reason."

They both looked at LuAnn, Tess waiting for her to refute the theory, Janice waiting for her to agree.

"I don't know." LuAnn finally lowered herself into the armchair opposite Tess. "It's possible."

It was possible that Jay was the wallet thief. Janice made a decent case, on the surface, and it would explain why he'd acted so strangely this afternoon and again tonight. He had been shocked then and uncomfortable now. But Tess had great points as well, and Janice's theory didn't seem to hold up under too much scrutiny.

"Maybe you've met him before somewhere, and he didn't want to remind you," Tess said. "An old boyfriend or something."

"He is definitely not an old boyfriend," LuAnn said.

"He's at least ten years older than she is," Janice said.

Tess shrugged. "Maybe she had a thing for older men at some point."

LuAnn tossed a throw pillow at her.

"Could it be an old teacher?" Janice asked. "Or someone from church?"

"Why wouldn't they just say hello in that case?" Tess asked. "If he's someone you knew at one point in your life, he doesn't seem to want to reconnect, based on what you're saying."

A pause, and then Janice said carefully, "Could it be someone who knew your father? Either before or after he disappeared?"

"I…" LuAnn didn't know what to say. She'd grown up believing that her father had abandoned her and her mother, but she'd recently discovered that he had actually been part of the Witness Protection Program and had disappeared in order to protect his family. "I don't know."

Every theory that they threw out sounded far fetched. And yet something *had* been off about Jay's reaction. Maybe it was because he'd stolen her wallet, but something in LuAnn said it was more than that. Something about him had unsettled her at

a deeper level. Something he'd said, something he'd done…
She didn't know what it was, but something about him felt
almost…familiar. As if she'd known him once. But for the life
of her, she couldn't figure out where, or when, or how.

She realized that Tess and Janice were waiting for her to say
something, so she decided it was a good time to change the
subject.

"Anyway. I had a good meeting with Brad today." LuAnn
reached for her notebook and flipped to the pages of scrawled
notes she'd taken that afternoon. "He thinks simple for the
flowers and table linens. And he said Lauren would prefer the
more American menu."

"Did he check with the bride on any of these things?"
Janice added another place card to her growing pile.

"He seems to think she'll be okay with whatever we put
together."

Janice didn't say anything.

"What?" LuAnn asked.

Janice took a deep breath and then said, "Lawrence did a
lot of weddings."

Lawrence was Janice's late husband. He'd been the pastor
of Christ Fellowship Church in Marietta before he passed away
a few years back. "Which means I dealt with a lot of brides. And
I never once met a bride who didn't have strong opinions about
every element of her wedding."

"You may be right," LuAnn said. "But this is what we have
to work with, and we don't have a lot of time. So unless we hear
differently from Brad, I'm not sure what else to do."

Janice nodded. "I see your point. I just hope Brad really is right about this."

"Me too." LuAnn looked down at her list. "He promised to get us the final list and final count by Wednesday. But it's around fifty. I'll place the order for the food tomorrow and have it delivered Thursday. I'll start cooking it that day, and hopefully it won't be a mad rush to get it all done Saturday."

"Which, again, would make it unlike any other wedding in history," Janice said with a small laugh.

"He did say they're not hiring a photographer, and so he hopes people take lots of photos that they can share," LuAnn said.

"Grant isn't going to take pictures for them?" Tess asked.

Brad's brother Grant was a photographer. Surely he'd give them a discounted rate.

"This wedding was so last-minute, he was already booked," LuAnn said.

"Well, I'm sure it won't be a problem to crowdsource photos. People these days can't seem to use the bathroom without putting it on social media," Janice said.

"It's true that most people will probably take pictures with their phones," Tess said. "But wouldn't it be fun to help them out a bit?"

"What do you mean?" Janice didn't sound suspicious exactly, but there was a question in her voice.

"I went to a wedding a few years back where they put disposable cameras at every place setting, and guests were encouraged to take pictures throughout the reception. The idea is, after the wedding, the bride and groom develop the film and are reminded of all the fun of the wedding."

"That is a cute idea," LuAnn said. "But can you even get disposable cameras anymore?"

Tess shrugged. "I did say it was a few years back. I think they have those cute Polaroid-like cameras now."

"I bet we could find something," Janice said. "I think that's a great idea. And what if we upped the ante and set up a photo booth? I saw one on Pinterest. You set up an area with a backdrop and lots of props, and people can take fun pictures."

"That's a cute idea," LuAnn said. "I bet they would love it. I'll ask Brad to see if Mark will spring for it."

They talked through more of the details for the wedding, and LuAnn assigned tasks. Soon the house was quiet, and Tess was yawning. "I think it's time for me to head to bed," she said, stretching her arms over her head.

"I'm right behind you," Janice said.

A few minutes later their rooms were dark, and LuAnn was climbing into bed. But she was jumpy, antsy. Her body was tired, but her mind was whirring, thinking through the strange day and all the questions that had been raised. She started to reach for the book that sat on her nightstand, but then she pushed herself out of bed and walked over to the closet. At the very back there were some boxes that she thought...

Aha. After a few moments of digging, she unearthed the box that contained her old high school yearbooks. She gathered them up and carried them to the bed. She only had two, from her junior and senior years. Her mom hadn't been able to afford the memento for the four years LuAnn had attended the school, and LuAnn had bought these two from her own earnings.

She flipped open the heavy cover of the book from her junior year and smiled, seeing the faces of so many old friends. Maryann had grandkids now, she knew, and still lived in Clarksburg. Patrick had joined the navy and was some kind of engineer. Kevin had died many years back, from complications of diabetes.

LuAnn studied each face as she flipped past, but none of them resembled Jay's. None of them triggered any sort of memory about how she'd met him before. With a sigh, she put the books aside, and her eyes lit on the stack of her mother's things she'd piled in the corner. There were some old diaries in there, written before LuAnn was born. She pushed herself out of bed and crouched down on the floor and pulled out a brown leather-bound diary. She flipped through it. Goodness. These entries were dated from before her mom had even married LuAnn's father.

LuAnn sat down on her bed again and flipped the delicate pages gently. Her mother's handwriting was so familiar. LuAnn pushed down the tears that sprang up. Oh dear. She still missed her, every single day, and as much as she loved seeing her mom's words on paper, as much as she loved getting to know what her mother had been like before LuAnn knew her, it still hurt to think of how much she'd lost.

LuAnn read through the entries, which started on Christmas Day, 1953, when her mom had been given the diary as a gift from her father. The first few entries detailed her mother's last semester of high school and her budding romance with Jasper, the captain of the football team she'd thought she was going to marry. Their dramatic breakup, just before prom, was recounted in detail, and LuAnn read greedily, drinking in the words. She'd once heard her mother mention a boyfriend from high school, but she'd never known much about this man who had broken her mother's heart. Was that heartache the reason she'd married LuAnn's father so quickly? Six months after high school graduation, she'd married Robert, and ten months after that LuAnn had been born.

LuAnn read about her mother's struggles during the early days of marriage and about her fear and excitement about becoming a mother. LuAnn loved reading how much her mother had adored Marietta, where they'd settled for LuAnn's father's job in 1954, and seeing the town through her mother's eyes, more than sixty years back, was sweet. And the pure, unadulterated love she had felt for her baby was clear, as was her frustration that more children didn't come as quickly or easily as LuAnn had. LuAnn had always known her mother had wanted more children, but reading the pain in her own words made LuAnn feel closer than ever to her.

After LuAnn's father left when she was six, her mom had taken LuAnn back home to West Virginia, living in a rural community outside of Charleston, not far from where she had grown up. She never said much about her husband's disappearance, which LuAnn now knew had been related to a crime he'd witnessed and not abandonment, as she had always believed. But she did recount much of the drama that played out when she returned home, child in tow, and much of the life in a country town was laid out on the page. LuAnn read about the time her grandfather got drunk on moonshine and fell off the chicken coop and broke his leg and about the family up the road who believed western medicine was the devil's work and treated every injury and illness with oils and herbs. She read about how her aunt Martha had run off with a deacon from their church and about the mining accident that had taken dozens of lives, including three members of her extended family. LuAnn remembered hearing about the huge cloud of smoke that had hovered over the town for days and the way people in town spoke about the accident in hushed tones for years afterward. And she read about her mom's friendship with Eleanor, the woman who led her mom to the Lord. Some of LuAnn's earliest memories were from their life in Clarksburg, and she enjoyed reliving some of these times through her mother's words.

There were so many things she hadn't known about her mother, like how she'd wanted to travel the world, to have a career of her own and wear suits to work. She hadn't been able to achieve any of those dreams, LuAnn realized with a sad sigh. How would her life have been different if she'd been born at a different time, in a different place? In rural West Virginia in the forties and fifties, women didn't do those things. But it made LuAnn smile to think that she'd had those dreams. LuAnn had always known her mother as a practical, logical woman, and now, after all this time, she was learning that there had been more to her than that. In some ways, reading these words, so personal and honest, felt like spying, but it also felt like getting to talk to her mother again.

Finally, her eyes started to feel heavy, and LuAnn set aside the diary and turned out the light. As she lay in bed, she tried to keep her mind focused on the image of her mother as a happy teenager, but her mind drifted back to the moment in the coffeehouse just after she'd spotted the man with his hand in her purse. Could it have been their guest after all? She rolled over, trying to picture him, trying to reconcile that image with the white-haired man staying in Moonlight and Snowflakes. It was hard to imagine. Then again, something was definitely off about Jay. Something about their conversation this evening was still nagging at LuAnn. Something about what he said. She played it back in her mind.

He had asked for some milk and had said whole was fine. He'd hardly said anything at all, actually, and yet she couldn't shake the feeling that something in his words had stuck out to her.

LuAnn turned back over, searching for a comfortable spot. Finally, as she started to drift off to sleep, she realized what it was.

It wasn't what Jay had said that had bothered her.

It was how he'd said it.

CHAPTER SIX

LuAnn woke up with a plan Tuesday morning. The sun was still coming up, casting a golden glow over the yard and the river. She made herself a cup of coffee in the Inn Crowd's small shared kitchen, then sat in the armchair by the window and spent some time reading her Bible and praying. She'd been reading through Psalms, finding comfort and beauty in the ancient poetry, and today the words of Psalm 46:10 resonated with her: *"Be still, and know that I am God."* There were always so many things to do just running the inn, let alone planning a wedding on top of it, and LuAnn's instinct was always to jump right into her day and all the things that needed to be done. It was nice to have the reminder to take a few moments and just sit, to just enjoy being in His presence.

After a while, she heard Janice stirring in her room, and LuAnn realized it was time to get ready to head downstairs. She quickly took a shower and dressed in light linen pants and a cotton blouse, and then she went to the kitchen, where Winnie was already working on a batch of blueberry pancakes. Something— a pan of muffins, LuAnn guessed—was in the oven.

"Good morning," she said.

"Good mornin'." Winnie looked up long enough to flash LuAnn a smile, then she turned back to the stove.

"What can I help you with?"

"You can get started on cutting up the fruit," Winnie said. LuAnn pulled out the colander and gently tossed in the blueberries, strawberries, and raspberries to rinse them. The berries had come fresh from the farmer's market yesterday. LuAnn loved the colors and flavors and textures. She sliced the strawberries and set them gently in a bowl and then layered in the other berries. She cut up a cantaloupe, adding the soft, peach-colored flesh to the salad. Then she went outside to the small garden by the back door and plucked a handful of mint leaves. She rinsed them, slivered them, and mixed them into the fruit.

By this time, Taylor had arrived for his morning shift, and guests were starting to make their way downstairs. LuAnn went out into the café and instructed them to sit wherever they liked. The café would open for business soon, and the scent of coffee and freshly baked pastries filled the room.

"Well, this is just delightful," one woman said. She and her husband had been wearing matching shirts the day before, and today they both wore white short-sleeved button-downs. Did they pack the same clothes for the whole trip? LuAnn wondered.

"Please, help yourselves to coffee. This morning's menu is on the chalkboard." LuAnn gestured toward the board on the wall.

"Ooh look, Robert, they have blueberry pancakes. And sausage! Oh, now what am I going to pick?" The enthusiastic woman turned back to LuAnn. "I just love everything about this place."

"I'm so glad to hear it."

The couple sat at a table by the window, and Taylor immediately approached with glasses of water and to ask if they had any questions about the menu. Taylor was a good hire, LuAnn thought. A student at Marietta College, he was reliable and dependable. He'd told her he'd been on the swim team in high school, and they had always practiced before school, so he was used to getting up early. She looked around the room now and saw that Jay and Jacqueline were coming down the stairs. She tried to keep her expression neutral as she approached them.

"Good morning," she said. "Did you sleep well?"

"Oh yes, we did, thank you. That bed is so comfortable," Jacqueline said. "And the view this morning! Seeing the sun come up over that river was stunning. I took a bunch of pictures, and I can't wait to show them to the ladies at the club—"

While Jacqueline chattered, LuAnn watched Jay's face. He didn't meet her eye, but he was composed and didn't have that same twitchy look he'd had the night before. Had something changed for him? Or did he, like LuAnn, wake up with a steely sense of purpose this morning?

"—smells so good. Oh look, they have blueberry pancakes. Jay, that's your favorite!"

Jacqueline was already dragging him toward a table, and LuAnn smiled and watched them go. She let them get settled and waited for Taylor to take their order, and then she casually wandered over to the coffee bar and poured herself a cup. She looked around the room, and then, as if the idea had just occurred to her, she wandered over to the table where Jay and

Jacqueline sat. She placed her hand on the back of an empty chair. "May I join you?"

"Of course! We'd love to have you." Jacqueline moved the sugar container and the salt and pepper shakers out of the way.

"So how are you enjoying Marietta so far? Did you enjoy the Campus Martius?" LuAnn had done some performing in college, and she tried to pretend she was just playing a part now—the part of a nosy innkeeper, as it turned out.

"Oh yes. I just love history," Jacqueline said. "It was so interesting. I had no idea it was the first fortification in the Northwest Territory."

LuAnn nodded, but she really wanted to hear Jay speak, and she suspected she might have to do some coaxing. She turned to him. "How about you, Jay? Did you enjoy it?"

"Oh yes," he said and then raised his coffee cup to his mouth. He took a sip, and in the silence that followed, his wife rushed to speak.

"Jay was in the army, so he always enjoys seeing places that have some kind of military connection."

"You were in the army?" LuAnn broke in before Jacqueline could continue. "When did you serve?"

Jay lowered his cup. "I joined up during Vietnam," he said. "And I got out in 1972."

"Thank you for your service," LuAnn said. She needed to keep him on this track. "And what about the rest of the town? I know you all had a bit of time to walk around before you checked in. Did you get a chance to see much?"

"Oh yes," Jacqueline said. "I found plenty of adorable little shops to explore."

"And she has the receipts to prove it," Jay said.

"I had to get souvenirs for the grandkids. You know how much Charlie likes trains."

She must have found a replica of the B&O trains that were on display over in Harmar Village. LuAnn turned to Jay. "And how about you? Did you shop too?"

She didn't expect him to just come out and admit he'd wandered into a coffeehouse and taken her wallet, but...Well, okay, maybe a small part of her was hoping he'd say something along those lines.

"Oh no, Jay doesn't do shopping," Jacqueline said.

"I wandered," Jay said.

"Did you see anything interesting?"

"Nothing that really sticks out." He shrugged and took another sip of coffee. "I went past some shops and walked along the river and then met up with Jacqueline for sandwiches I got from a little café."

Was he being intentionally vague? Or was this the way he normally spoke? She decided she was going to have to be direct.

"Did you make it to Jeremiah's? It's this cute little coffee-house over on Front Street. They have great iced coffee. Nothing better on a hot day."

"No." He lifted his mug to his lips and took another sip. "I'm afraid I didn't make it there."

"Jay just loves to walk. He can't sit still," Jacqueline said. "Usually he runs every morning, but on a tour like this it's hard. So he wanders. I learned long ago to let him go off and do his thing and get some energy out, and it leaves me in peace to browse the places I want to see without him looking over my shoulder."

She gave her husband a fond smile and picked up the sugar container. She dumped some sugar into her coffee and stirred it.

"Wow, a runner? That's so impressive!" LuAnn looked at Jay. He was rather fit, she now realized. Thin, but you could see defined muscles in his arms under his polo shirt. But he had to be in his seventies.

"I know, it's crazy right? That's what I think too. But he loves it. He runs 10Ks and half marathons."

"It's been a few years since I ran a half marathon," Jay said, shaking his head. "I do like to run, but these days my runs are a lot slower and shorter than they used to be."

"That's amazing. The last time I went for a run, it was to get to the donut shop before it closed," LuAnn joked. Jacqueline laughed, and Jay let out a chuckle too.

"It keeps me out of trouble," he said. LuAnn was going to ask him another question, but just then Taylor arrived with a plate in each hand. He set a plate of blueberry pancakes in front of Jay and a serving of eggs and sausage in front of Jacqueline.

"Well now, this looks delicious." Jacqueline unfolded her napkin and set it in her lap.

"So, you're from Kentucky?" LuAnn said.

"Born and bred," Jacqueline answered.

"She's a real Southern belle," Jay said. "Finishing school, cotillion, hats at the derby, the works."

"Oh, hush." His wife laughed good-naturedly. "Cotillion is not that strange." She turned to LuAnn. "My family has owned a horse farm for generations."

"That sounds lovely." LuAnn pictured rolling green hills and split-rail fences and copper-maned horses.

"It really was a wonderful childhood. And I have a big family, so there were always lots of people around. We're still close, and we enjoy spending a lot of time with them."

"And I'm guessing from your feelings about cotillion that you're not from a horse farming family," LuAnn said to Jay. "Where did you grow up?" Tess had told her what she'd found out last night, but LuAnn wanted to hear it from his own mouth.

"No, I did not grow up raising horses," he said. "I'm from just outside Columbus. Think more urban blight than horse farm. It's been an interesting experience seeing how the other half lives."

He said it with such a practiced, even tone that she almost believed him. Almost.

"Oh, hush." Jacqueline said again, smacking him with her napkin. "Jay just likes to—"

Just then, a little dinging sound rang out. Someone was tapping a spoon against a glass. LuAnn looked up and saw that Meaghan was standing at the front of the café.

"Sorry to interrupt, but we'll be leaving in ten minutes for the Ohio River Museum. So if you'd like to get back to your room to finish getting ready for the day, now is the time." She used the same calm, level voice she seemed to always employ. She was wearing black skinny jeans and a flowy flowered top today, and she held her clipboard in one hand and a cup of coffee in the other.

"Well, I guess we'd better get going," Jacqueline said and pushed herself up. LuAnn wanted to ask more questions, but she saw that her opportunity had passed, as Jay also stood. "Thank you so much for chatting with us."

"Before you go—" LuAnn had to be bold. "I just can't help thinking you look so familiar, Jay. Have we met before?"

"No," he said, shaking his head. "I can't say I believe so." Had it come out just a little too fast? Like he'd been prepared with the answer?

"People are always thinking that about Jay," Jacqueline said. "He has this friendly face, and people always seem to think they know him."

It was more than that, something inside LuAnn knew. But now they were rushing off to be gone for their day, and LuAnn couldn't think of any good way to stop them. She waved as they headed up the stairs and watched until they disappeared around the bend of the hallway. She hadn't gotten the chance to ask everything she'd wanted to, but she'd learned a few things, and she'd gotten Jay to warm up to her a bit. He hadn't turned white and stared at her this time, and by the end of their visit, she would even say he had become almost downright chatty. And she'd determined one thing for sure. No matter what he said, Jay was not from Columbus, Ohio.

Janice had come downstairs sometime during their conversation, and by the time they'd helped Taylor clear the tables, it was time to open the café for breakfast customers. LuAnn was kept a bit busier than usual, because customers kept asking her about the theft of her wallet. She didn't understand what the fuss was about until she took a cup of coffee to Tess at the check-in desk and found her reading the morning's paper.

"Look, LuAnn, you're famous."

LuAnn set Tess's mug down and took a sip from her own. "What?"

Tess flipped to the second page of the newspaper, where there were often small local news items listed. "'A woman's wallet was stolen from her bag after she stepped away from it in Jeremiah's Coffee House Monday,'" Tess read. "'The victim was identified as LuAnn Sherrill, of Marietta. Police responded to the scene, but the perpetrator, who was described as tall and wearing a blue shirt, khakis, and a straw hat, has not been found.'"

"Oh dear." LuAnn sighed as Janice joined them. "I guess now everyone knows what an idiot I am."

"Don't worry about it," Janice said. For a moment, LuAnn feared she was about to say that everyone already knew what an idiot she was, but then she realized Janice would never say something that mean. "Hopefully getting the news out will mean they find the guy."

"Let's hope so." LuAnn was supposed to receive a replacement credit card in the mail today. She would need to get a new wallet and order a new driver's license and a new library card, but hopefully she could get that all squared away quickly.

"You seemed to be having an interesting conversation before the tour group left," Janice said to LuAnn. "How were Jay and Jacqueline this morning?"

"They were just fine." She saw the pointed look in Janice's eyes and knew what she was really asking. "As I was falling asleep last night, I realized what it was that was bothering me about Jay."

"And it wasn't the fact that he was clearly spooked by you?" Tess asked.

"Not exactly," LuAnn said. "It was how he spoke."

"What do you mean?"

"He told you he was from Ohio, right?" she said to Tess. Tess nodded.

"I asked him again this morning, just to hear him say it himself. And he told me he was from outside Columbus."

"Okay…" Tess was clearly waiting for the other shoe to drop.

"But he's not from Columbus. There's no way. He's from West Virginia, or Virginia, or somewhere thereabouts."

"What makes you say that?" Tess asked.

LuAnn took another sip. "I spent most of my life in West Virginia. There's a particular accent there, and I hear it in Jay's speech." She tilted her head to the side. "Do you remember the narrator from *The Waltons*? Earl…something. He had that Virginia lilt to his voice, remember? If you listen carefully, Jay has the same lilt. Not all the time, but enough. I've grown used to hearing it, so it's second nature to me—I think that's why I couldn't figure out right away what it was about Jay that was bugging me."

Janice pointed at LuAnn. "Earl Hamner Jr.," she said. Janice was their resident *Little House on the Prairie/Waltons/ Dr. Quinn* expert. "But you don't have an accent."

"I spent most of my time in Clarksburg, which is a big city." LuAnn thought about her trips to Rome, Berlin, and Barcelona. "Well, big for West Virginia anyway," she amended. "But my mother's side of the family is from the rural part of the state, way north and west. That's pure Appalachia there, and the farther you get up into those hills, the more pronounced the accent gets. And Jay has it."

"What do you mean?" Tess set the paper down. "I don't hear it."

"It's not obvious. I've just picked up on it on a few words. But it's more than just the words…It's something I can't explain. It's just…an Appalachian accent."

"Huh." Janice shook her head.

"What does that mean?" LuAnn asked.

"It means I'm thinking," Janice said. "Why would he lie about that?"

"I have no idea," LuAnn said.

"His wife seems to think he's from Ohio," Tess said. "She's the one who told me that last night. Are you saying Jacqueline is lying too?"

"I'm not sure exactly what I'm saying," LuAnn admitted. "I'm just pointing out that I don't buy that part of his story."

"And that, on top of the strange way he reacted when he saw you yesterday, is making you suspicious," Tess said.

LuAnn nodded. "But suspicious of what?" She shrugged. "I'm not sure."

"I still think he must be the one who took your wallet," Janice said. "And that he and his wife must have concocted a story about who they really are."

LuAnn considered this. It was still a possibility, even if it wasn't at all probable. And the fact that Jay was a runner made it slightly more plausible, she supposed. But had he and Jacqueline really made up a story about who they were? Had Jacqueline really not grown up on a horse farm and danced at a cotillion? It had seemed so convincing. It was possible, she supposed. If LuAnn was going to make up a childhood in Kentucky, it would no doubt include horse farms and debutante balls. *Had* she simply made it all up? LuAnn didn't have any way to know. But something told her Jay's strange reaction to her went deeper than a stolen wallet. That Jacqueline hadn't made up a whole childhood to cover for a stolen forty dollars.

"Is it possible he's someone you knew in West Virginia? Maybe someone you taught with?" Tess asked.

"I guess it's possible..." But wouldn't she remember a colleague, even one ten or fifteen years older than she was? "I looked through my old yearbooks last night, and he's not someone I went to school with. I suppose he could be someone I taught with." But why wouldn't he acknowledge the connection in that case?

"Or maybe it's someone from your church?" Tess added. "Maybe someone you saw every week but didn't really know?"

LuAnn thought back to the church she'd attended in Clarksburg. It had been a recently built modern building on the outskirts of town, with padded pews and a high-tech sound booth and drop-down screens for projecting the words to the songs. She hadn't known everybody in the church. It was possible. But then…she didn't think so. However she knew Jay, it wasn't from something recent. It was from long ago. "It doesn't feel right."

"No?" Tess's mouth curved downward. "How about your church growing up?"

LuAnn pictured the little white wooden building nestled in the foothills on the outskirts of town. Charleston was the state capital, and it had a pretty little downtown area with the iconic golden dome of the capital building. But once you left that area, it got rural quickly. LuAnn and her mother had rented a little apartment over a garage at the bottom of a hill, just a quick drive from the diner, and the church they had gone to drew mostly from the immediate area. She had felt at home in that small church and had known just about everyone in the tight-knit church community. And yet it was possible, she supposed, that someone she'd known as a child remembered her, even if she had no memory of him.

"It feels more right than the idea that I knew him as an adult," she finally said.

Tess shook her head. "The problem here is too many feelings."

Janice tilted her head and wrinkled her brow at her.

"You keep saying 'that doesn't feel right' or 'that feels possible.' But we don't need feelings. What we need are facts. Evidence."

It was so unlike Tess that LuAnn had to pay attention. "What do you mean?"

"I mean, we need to stop guessing about who Jay really is and figure it out."

"And how do you propose to do that?" Janice asked.

Tess opened the drawer in the desk where they'd stuck the packet of information Meaghan had handed them about the guests on the Thatch tour. "We'll start with this."

She pulled out the packet and flipped to the page with the photocopy of Jay's and Jacqueline's driver's licenses. She pointed out Jay's Kentucky license. "This has his home address and date of birth," she said. "That should give us a place to start."

Janice took the iPad from the desk drawer, opened a browser window, and typed in the address listed on his license. Several links popped up, and Janice touched the first, a real estate site that showed a big white house on a hill surrounded by lawn. The house didn't appear to be for sale, but for a price you could see the sales history. Next to the picture was an estimate of what the property would sell for. Tess's mouth dropped open.

"That much? For that house?"

"It's on seven acres," LuAnn pointed out.

"But still." Janice shook her head. "Wow. Why would he be picking pockets if he could afford something like that?"

"This tour they're on must cost more than my first house," Tess said. "I don't think money is the motivation if he's behind the wallet theft." She sounded dubious. LuAnn guessed that Janice was the only one who still held on to that theory at this point. Tess turned to LuAnn. "Does this look at all familiar to you? Or give you any clue as to how you might know him?"

LuAnn shook her head. "I've driven through Kentucky, but I've never been to the Lexington area. And I've never seen that house before."

Just then Taylor came out of the café, his backpack slung over his shoulder, and LuAnn realized how late it was getting.

"Have a good day," she called.

"Thanks." Taylor waved to them, and then he disappeared out the front door.

"We should get started on tidying the rooms while the group is out," Tess said.

"I've got to get back to those place cards for the wedding," Janice said. "You probably didn't see it yet, but Brad sent an updated list."

"And I need to get that food order placed so there's something to eat at the wedding," LuAnn said.

Janice tucked the iPad back in the desk, and all three reluctantly went back to their tasks. LuAnn went into the small office and logged into the computer. She tried to focus on the food order, but her mind was elsewhere, searching the hills and hollows of West Virginia in her mind, hoping to find any scrap of a memory that would explain why she felt so certain that no matter what he'd said, she'd met Jay before.

CHAPTER SEVEN

August 24, 1859

"Come in, come in." Anna Barton gestured for Prudence to step inside. "Let me take a look at thee. Is thee eating enough? Thee looks too thin. Now, let me see that little one. Oh, my word. He's precious. He's grown so much, hasn't he?"

Before Prudence could answer any of Anna's questions, Anna had taken Moses from her arms and was holding him up, his chubby little legs dangling beneath him. His face brightened into a smile.

As Anna bustled around her, ushering her into a chair and setting the kettle on to make tea, Prudence felt the strain of the journey start to melt away. The little house wasn't much, but it felt like home. These four walls had provided her shelter and stability when she had been in desperate need of both.

After Prudence had escaped from slavery, when her parents decided she should take a risk for her freedom, she'd ended up tired and hungry and sick and nearing a state of delirium that would have certainly meant the end of her. She was found by a Quaker man who brought her to Anna, and

Anna took her in and nursed her back to health. Anna eventually adopted her, giving her a new name and a home and a faith that had shaped the course of her life.

The house hadn't changed much. The walls were still bare, except for a small cross-stitched sampler that said "The Lord is My Shepherd." The furniture was sparse but sturdy. The little pallet in the corner where Prudence had slept next to Anna's bed had been replaced by a braided rug, but otherwise there was little change.

"It is wonderful to see thee." Anna handed back baby Moses, and Prudence took him gratefully. Then Anna moved to the stove and tended the kettle of boiling water. "But given how busy thee is with the farm and the babe, I wonder that thee could spare the time."

Anna was grayer than last time Prudence had been to visit, and the lines around her mouth a bit more set. But her perceptiveness and her intuition were as strong as ever.

"I did want to see thee, of course," Prudence started. "And I know thee is anxious to see Moses. I want him to grow up knowing thee, knowing this place."

Prudence was working her way around to asking the question she didn't know how to speak out loud.

"Child." Anna straightened and brushed her hands against the apron tied at her waist. "Thee is welcome here, anytime, in any circumstance. No matter what."

"Thank thee." And even though Prudence knew that, at her core, just hearing the words spoken aloud was enough to make her eyes well up with tears. It felt so good to be here, to be loved, unconditionally. And that made it all the harder to ask what she had come here to ask.

"But I did wonder if there wasn't some reason thee came today," Anna continued. "Some reason that thee was able to get away."

Prudence adjusted Moses on her lap. He was more alert these days and loved to rest on her lap and look around, so she settled him there now.

"In fact, there is something I want to ask thee," Prudence said.

Anna nodded, indicating she should go on.

"I just wondered..." Prudence took a deep breath. She did not want to hurt Anna, but wasn't sure there was any other choice. "I thought I remembered that thee once tried to locate my family. My..." "Real" wasn't the right word—Anna was as real as family came—"My birth family."

Anna took a deep breath, and then she lowered herself down onto the bench next to the table. How many meals had Prudence eaten at that table?

"I wondered if that was it," she said. "It's only natural, now that thee has got the little one, to wonder about thy own parents."

"It's not that I don't thank thee—"

Anna held up a hand to wave her words away. "I know. Child, I know." She shook her head and then continued. "I did try to find them, many years ago, when thee first arrived. Mind, it wasn't because I didn't want thee here. When thee showed up here, it was..." She took a deep, jagged breath. "It changed everything for me."

Prudence nodded. When Prudence had been brought here, Anna's husband had recently passed away from scarlet fever. The child for whom they had prayed for years had never come. In so many ways, the two of them, Prudence and Anna, had helped each other, though Prudence hadn't realized that until many years later.

"I did not want to find them, if I am being honest," Anna said. "I was afraid that if they were alive, I would lose thee."

"Thee would never—"

"I know that now. I did not know it then. But I felt I had to try, for thy sake. If thy family was still out there, I had to try to find them for thee."

Prudence didn't know what to say, so she simply nodded again.

"Thee had said thee was from an area in the hills near to a town called Sneedville, so I wrote to the Quaker church nearest to there, asking if anyone knew of a Collins family."

Collins had been Prudence's birth name. Effie Collins.

"My people were not Quaker," Prudence said. Her parents had been Christians, but she had only come to know a personal relationship with God and His saving role in her life once she'd come to live with Anna.

"I know that, sweet child. I mentioned in my letter that thy people were Melungeon." Prudence's people were usually darker skinned than she was. Gypsies, some called them. Descended from African slaves, others said. Prudence did not know. All she knew was that her people had a life and a culture all their own, but the slave traders and plantation owners had not understood it.

"I also mentioned that thee had lived out in the hills, from what thee told me of thy early days."

The rolling hills and steeply pitched valleys that had been the landscape of her childhood were imprinted on her soul. Prudence—Effie—would never forget the freedom of roaming around those hills, of the warmth on her skin in the summer or the biting wind in the winter.

"Thee didn't hear a response though." Prudence knew it to be true. Her people kept themselves separate. They kept to themselves. Well, they preferred it that way. It had seemed safer that way. Until one day it wasn't.

Prudence took in a deep breath. She did not like to remember that day.

"I did hear back, but the answer was that the church did not know of a Collins family."

Even though Prudence had expected it, the news still stung. Though they had lived near her mother's family, her father's people were not from the area. She and her parents were the only Collinses around.

"It had been too many years," Anna said gently. "From what the Quaker church understood, most of the Melungeon families were gone by that point. Scattered."

That made sense as well. After the raid where Effie and her family had been captured, anyone who had escaped would have likely left the area. And just like that, their whole community had been destroyed. All because of the greed of—

No. She could not allow herself to wallow there. She had to work on forgiving. She had to—

"But after many letters, I did get one piece of hopeful information," Anna continued. "Someone from the church rode out to the area where the Melungeons had lived, just to see, and I was told that there was a woman named Alice who still lived out that way."

Prudence's breath caught. Alice. Surely it couldn't be—

"The Quaker man who had gone out to see told me she would not come to the door. She was inside, he could hear her moving around, but she would not answer the door to him. Which, I guess, I can probably understand. She probably did not trust the light-skinned man at her door."

"I would imagine not," Prudence said. But still, if Alice had survived, maybe she knew something.

"I wrote to this Alice many times, but I never received an answer," Anna continued. "I do not know if the letters ever made it to her or not."

There was not a reliable mail delivery system out in those hills, Prudence knew. It consisted mainly of people passing letters as they rode through town. It was possible that Alice had never gotten the letters. Or, she thought with a sigh, it was possible that she had, and simply had not wanted to or been able to respond.

"I thank thee for trying so hard."

Now that Prudence was a mother, she understood what it had surely cost Anna to try to find her adopted daughter's family. If she succeeded, it likely would have meant giving Prudence up, and by that point the runaway Melungeon slave girl had become Anna's whole world. Prudence was not sure she would have had the courage to write those letters herself.

"Short of going out there myself to knock on her door, I wasn't sure what to do to get in touch with her," Anna said. "And bear in mind, that was many years ago. I do not know if she is still there."

"What address did thee use?"

"I can dig it up," Anna said. "Did thee know this Alice?"

Prudence adjusted Moses on her lap. "She was my aunt. My mother's oldest sister. She was…She was away the day of the raid."

"Oh, child." Anna looked like she wanted to say more, but instead she bit her lip. "I'm so sorry."

"I would like to write to her," Prudence said.

"Of course."

Prudence did not know whether her aunt Alice would ever get her letter, let alone remember her and know anything about what had happened to her parents. But still, as she sat in this snug cabin with the woman who had become her family, Prudence felt the closest thing to hope she'd felt in a long time.

CHAPTER EIGHT

After LuAnn placed the grocery order for the wedding, she checked the mail and found that her new credit card had arrived. She tucked it into her purse and debated going out to buy herself a new wallet, but she still held out hope that her old wallet would be returned, so she decided to wait. In the meantime, she would start on the day's laundry. But as she neared the door to the basement, the inn's phone rang, and she went back to answer it.

"Hello?" It was a local number, but not one she recognized. Maybe it was the police calling with good news. "Wayfarers Inn."

"LuAnn?"

She recognized the voice immediately, and she felt her hopes vanish.

"Hello, Thelma." Thelma Bickerton was one of Brad's great-aunts. She and her sister Irene lived in a stately historic home on one of the nicest streets in Marietta. The two were tough and proud and could always be counted on to know the latest happenings in town. "How are you?"

"I'm doing just fine, thank you very much." At ninety-five, Thelma was no spring chicken, but LuAnn had never heard her complain about her health. "I wanted to make sure you'd heard about what happened at the River Museum."

"I haven't," LuAnn said. What in the world was she talking about? "What happened?"

"Another wallet was stolen." It was clear from her tone that Thelma relished being the one to share the news. "From an unattended bag, just like yours."

"Really?"

"It's true. From just outside the gift shop. It's terrible, isn't it?"

She didn't sound like she thought it was terrible, but LuAnn let that go.

"What happened? When was this?"

"This morning. Just a little while ago."

"Whose wallet was it?"

"You know Jody McMaster?"

"Yes, I think so." LuAnn had first met Jody at the informational meeting the bank had held about the plans for the inn before she and Tess and Janice had bought the building. Jody had taught with Janice for years, LuAnn recalled.

"Her daughter Lindsay is in town, and they went there this morning with Lindsay's two-year-old. Apparently the wallet was in the diaper bag, which they left draped over the stroller just outside the gift shop."

"I'm so sorry to hear that." Her mind was racing. Could it be...? Surely it wasn't the same person who had—

"Yes, well, since it happened so quickly after you were pick-pocketed, we thought you might want to know."

"I..." LuAnn wasn't sure what to say. "Thank you for letting me know, I guess."

"Tell her about the hat," LuAnn heard Irene say in the background.

"Someone saw a man in a straw hat," Thelma continued. "Isn't that the description you gave as well?"

"I...Yes, that's right."

Thelma made an undecipherable noise in response.

LuAnn waited for her to say more, but Thelma didn't go on. "Thank you for letting me know," LuAnn said again.

"I guess we'll all be smart enough not to leave bags unattended anymore," Thelma said in response.

"Yes, I guess we will." And then, because she wasn't sure what else to say, she added, "Have a great day."

Thelma made another noise in response, and LuAnn hung up, thinking through what Thelma had said. If it was true—and surely it was; Thelma and Irene knew most of what went on in this town, and they wouldn't have gotten something like this wrong—it meant that whoever had taken her wallet had struck again. And...LuAnn hated this thought. Hadn't the tour group been heading to the Ohio River Museum this morning?

LuAnn put the phone down and took the elevator to the top floor, where she found Janice sitting on the couch flipping through bridal magazines.

"Finding anything useful?" she asked Janice.

Janice set the magazine down. "I suppose. I was looking at cakes. We need to place the order at the bakery today if we have any hope of getting it in time for Saturday." They had toyed with the idea of having LuAnn and Winnie bake the cake, but with all the other food that needed to be prepared for the wedding, it seemed like that was a task better left to the professionals. "And that's only if they take pity on us. I know you said Lauren wants something simple, but I still want it to be beautiful." She ran a hand through her platinum curls. "But mostly I'm just finding how over-the-top everything wedding is these days. Have you seen these 'I said yes to the dress' photos?"

"The what?"

"Apparently you're supposed to bring a chalkboard or some other writing surface with you when you go dress shopping so when you find the right dress, you can write 'I said yes to the dress!' and hold it and have a picture taken so you can post it on Instagram."

"I had no idea."

"It seems most of what happens in weddings these days is designed around what will look good on Instagram."

"Goodness." LuAnn had never been married, but she'd gotten close. Her fiancé had died just weeks before they were set to be married, so she had been through the process of planning a wedding. "That seems to miss the point, doesn't it?"

"I'm afraid it does." Janice shook her head. "Anyway, that's not why you came up here. You look like you have something to say."

"Unfortunately, I have bad news." LuAnn sat down in an armchair across from Janice. "Thelma Bickerton just called."

"Oh dear. That is bad news."

LuAnn laughed. "She wanted to let me know that a wallet was just taken at the Ohio River Museum."

"Oh no." She could see that Janice understood what this meant. "Wasn't the tour group going to—"

"That's right."

"Oh, but—"

"I know." LuAnn took a breath and continued. "She told me it was Jody McMaster's daughter whose wallet was taken."

"Lindsay is in town?" Janice perked up immediately. "Jody must be so thrilled. She just loves that little grandbaby. Lindsay only lives in Cleveland, but she doesn't make it home nearly enough for Jody's taste, especially now with Carter. I bet they're having—" Janice's face changed, and then she stopped. "Oh, how awful."

"I thought you might want to know, since she's your friend and all."

"I do, thanks." Janice pushed herself up. "All right then. Do you need a few minutes to get ready, or are you set to go now?"

"Go where?"

Janice looked at her like she was speaking a foreign language. "To talk to Jody and Lindsay, of course. And then to the police station."

LuAnn understood. Janice wanted to find out about the robbery. "Give me five minutes."

Fifteen minutes later, they were pulling up in front of Jody McMaster's Craftsman-style bungalow on Eighth Street. There was a covered porch and a small terrace off the second floor, and the pitched roof and square, boxy construction gave the house charm. Janice parked on the brick road, and they made their way up the wide expanse of green lawn. The day was hot and sunny, and LuAnn enjoyed the feeling of the warm sun on her skin.

LuAnn was dubious about this visit. After what had to have been a trying morning, she was certain the last thing Jody would want would be a visit, but Janice insisted that she would be glad to see them when she understood the reason.

Janice clutched a plate of Winnie's lemon cookies that were always a hit with their guests, and LuAnn rang the doorbell.

"Janice," Jody said as she opened the door. Jody had short gray hair and thick-framed glasses. "Hello there. And LuAnn. It's good to see you."

"Hi there," Janice said. "We're sorry to bother you, but we heard you had a bad morning."

"Oh yes." She smiled and looked down at the plate of cookies. "Please come on in."

She stepped back, and they stepped inside. It was cool and quiet inside, and though the home was tastefully decorated in shades of blue, there were toys strewn everywhere.

"Excuse the mess," Jody said, gesturing at the miniature trucks and cars all across the floor. "Carter is very into vehicles at the moment." She gestured for them to sit on a white couch, which LuAnn quickly surmised had not been purchased with a toddler in mind. She took in a bookshelf packed with classics, the spines well-worn, and a collection of family photos on the mantel. Jody took the plate of cookies, and they sat down. "I guess you're here about Lindsay's wallet?"

"Yes," said Janice. "We were so sorry to hear about what happened."

"Lindsay's just putting Carter down for a nap now, but she'll be out in a minute, and I'm sure she'll be glad to tell you about it." Jody peeled the cling wrap off the plate of cookies and set it down on a steamer trunk piled with books that served as a coffee table. Janice had never said what Jody taught at the high school, but between the books and the throw pillow with the C.S. Lewis quote, *"You can never get a cup of tea large enough or a book long enough to suit me,"* LuAnn guessed English.

"I read about your wallet being taken in the paper this morning," Jody continued. "We should have known better, but that gift store is so small and crowded, and it seemed better to leave the stroller outside."

"Believe me, I understand how easy it is to make a mistake like that," LuAnn said.

"Ah. Lindsay, can you come in here?"

They looked up as a woman in shorts and a T-shirt came down the hall. She had the same high cheekbones as her mom, but her hair was lighter.

"Yeah?" She looked around the room and noticed Janice. "Oh. Hello, Mrs. Eastman."

"Hello, Lindsay." Janice smiled warmly. "It's nice to see you. Congratulations on the baby."

"Thank you. Only he's not such a baby anymore, more an impossible toddler."

"I understand that." Janice gestured toward LuAnn. "This is my friend LuAnn Sherrill. We run an inn in town, along with our friend Tess."

"Ah. Right. You're the one whose wallet was taken." Lindsay sat down on the couch next to her mom. "Well, the other one now, I guess."

"Exactly." LuAnn sighed. "I was hoping to find out if you caught a glimpse of the thief or saw anyone around or anything like that."

"I'm afraid not," Lindsay said. "I had taken Carter into the children's exhibit and brought the stroller with me in there, but the gift shop is so tiny. There's no room for a giant stroller in there."

"Have you seen the size of strollers these days?" Jody said. "Bigger than a small car."

"Which is why I try not to carry both a diaper bag and a purse on top of it," Lindsay said. "I had tucked my wallet and phone into the diaper bag, and I left it outside the gift shop thinking it would be fine there. This is small-town Ohio, right? I was only a few feet away, and most people don't willingly go rooting around in a diaper bag."

"You never know what you're going to find," Jody said, nodding.

LuAnn laughed, and Lindsay continued. "I wasn't planning to buy anything, but Mom wanted to look around—"

"You can't pass up the gift shop," Jody said.

"—and when we were in there, Carter saw those stuffed cardinals they carry..." Her voice trailed upward.

The cardinal was the state bird of Ohio. Many shops carried them in various forms.

"So when I went back to get my wallet to buy the thing, it was gone."

"The diaper bag was gone?" Janice asked.

Lindsay shook her head. "Just the wallet. Everything else was there."

"That's strange," LuAnn said. "Was the wallet visible?"

"I don't know." Lindsay sighed. "I thought I tucked it down in there, but whoever it was might have been able to see it, I guess."

"Did you see anyone near the stroller?"

"I didn't," Lindsay said. "There were so many people around."

"There was a big tour group, along with the regular visitors," Jody added. "And we weren't really paying attention to it, because we were focused on Carter."

"Of course," LuAnn said. It made sense, but it didn't help her much.

"One woman said she'd been standing outside the gift shop and had seen a man near the stroller, but she didn't see him touch it."

"Did she describe the man?"

"She said he had a white shirt and a hat. But she didn't actually see him take anything."

LuAnn looked at Janice. Jay had been wearing a white shirt that morning. "Did she say how old he was?"

"She thought he was older, but she couldn't say." Lindsay shrugged.

"The woman, I should point out, was probably in her twenties," Jody said. "So anyone over thirty is old."

"Did anyone else notice anything?" Janice asked.

"When the police arrived, they asked anyone who was around if they'd seen anything, but by then most of the people who had been near the gift shop had moved on. They said it wasn't a lot to go on."

"What about security cameras?" LuAnn asked. Surely the museum would have those, especially near the gift shop.

"The staff was going to pull the footage and give it to the police," Jody said. "We haven't heard whether it provided any clues yet. They said they'd get us a copy of it."

There was a crash, followed by a cry, from the back of the house. Lindsay bolted out of the room before LuAnn had even registered what it was.

"Carter isn't used to sleeping in a bed," Jody explained.

"Oh dear." Janice's face pinched in concern.

"It's okay. It's already happened a few times this visit. We put pillows down on the floor. He'll be fine."

LuAnn wanted to laugh at how nonchalant she was, especially compared to Lindsay's reaction, but instead, she stood. "You've been very helpful," she said. "Thank you for talking with us."

"Of course." Jody stood and walked them to the door. "Please let us know if you hear anything about your wallet."

"We will. And enjoy the rest of your time with your daughter," LuAnn said. Jody thanked them, and they stepped back out into the sunshine.

"It was him," Janice said. "He was wearing a white shirt today! And they were there. The tour group was there!"

"Maybe." LuAnn had to agree that it did seem pretty coincidental that the theft had happened at just the time when Jay and the rest of the Thatch tour group were visiting the museum. But that didn't prove anything. And lots of people wore white shirts. "But I think we need to see that security video footage."

"I was thinking the same thing," Janice said.

They climbed back into Janice's car and pulled up in front of the Marietta police station a few minutes later. The station was housed in a two-story brick building set back from the road and surrounded by a lush lawn and trees. They parked in the lot at the side of the building and made their way up the stone walkway to the front entrance.

Inside, they approached the front desk. The station was dark and cool, and behind the imposing front desk there was a window with reinforced glass and a door that led to the back. A man who was probably in his fifties, with a sizable paunch and a thick mustache, was seated at the desk. He looked up from the computer screen when they approached.

"Hello," LuAnn said. "We're hoping to talk to Chief Mayfield or Officer Lewis."

"What is this regarding?" he said in a lazy drawl.

"It's about the wallet that was stolen today at the Ohio River Museum," LuAnn said.

"Hold on, please."

He picked up the phone on his desk and made a call, and then he set the phone down again. "Chief Mayfield says to come on back. Second floor. Second door on the right."

The door beside the desk started to buzz, and LuAnn realized he was unlocking it. She walked forward and pulled the door open, and then she and Janice walked into the back. There was an open space where several officers were hunched over desks or staring at screens, and beyond that was a wall with an elevator. They walked over and Janice pushed the button for the elevator, and the doors swished open. A moment later they stepped out into a hallway on the second floor and then walked down to the second door on the right side. The door was partly closed, so LuAnn knocked gently.

"Come in."

She pushed open the door and found Chief Mayfield seated behind a desk. A big window on the far wall let in lots of sunlight, and on the wall next to his desk were awards and photos of the police chief with various minor celebrities.

"Hello, LuAnn, Janice." He stood up and shook their hands and gestured for them to sit in the chairs across from his desk.

"Hi, Chief Mayfield," LuAnn said. "How are you?"

"I'm good. What can I help you with?" He held a brass-colored pen in one hand and used it to doodle on a notepad in front of him.

"We were wondering if you had any information on the missing wallet," LuAnn said.

"Or if there was anything you could tell us about the wallet theft this morning," Janice added.

Chief Mayfield let out a slow breath. "News does travel quickly around these parts, doesn't it?"

"Oh, it's all the way around town and back by now," Janice said. "Thelma Bickerton called LuAnn, what, almost an hour and a half ago now? It's safe to say most people this side of the Ohio River know about it."

"I'm afraid there's not much I can tell you." Chief Mayfield was drawing a sequence of interconnected squares on his notepad. "Naturally we suspect the thefts are linked, but we don't have any solid evidence connecting them."

"How about suspects?" LuAnn asked.

"We're working on it."

LuAnn caught Janice's eye and shook her head slightly. As much as she wanted to get to the truth, and even though today's incident moved him back onto the suspect list, it would be terrible if they brought up Jay, and he turned out to be innocent. Talk about bad for business—they'd probably never recover from the negative PR.

"What about the security camera footage?" LuAnn asked. "Lindsay told us the footage exists."

"You've already spoken to Lindsay?" Chief Mayfield stopped doodling and looked up at them.

"We do have a vested interest in finding the wallet thief," LuAnn said.

"We've got our team reviewing it," Chief Mayfield said.

"You wouldn't happen to have an extra copy of the footage available, would you?" Janice asked.

"I'm afraid not. I can't give you a copy of the footage," Chief Mayfield said.

LuAnn had suspected as much, but it didn't hurt to ask. Still, she had every intention of finding a way to take a look at it.

"I can assure you, we are taking this very seriously," Chief Mayfield said. "And we are doing everything we can to find your wallet."

"I do appreciate it." LuAnn slowly pushed herself up from her chair. She did believe that they were working on it. But she certainly wasn't going to sit around and wait for them to solve the mystery.

CHAPTER NINE

When they got back to the inn, they found Tess hunched over a laptop in their sitting room on the fourth floor.

"How did it go?" Tess asked without looking up from the screen. LuAnn looked at Janice. She wasn't sure how to answer. They hadn't learned anything they could report, exactly. But more than that, LuAnn was flummoxed to see Tess sitting here in the middle of the day. Even though Robin and Taylor and Winnie were handling the café lunch crowd today, none of the Inn Crowd spent much time sitting around surfing the internet.

"It was..." Janice said, meeting LuAnn's eye. Her eyebrow was raised. She was surprised too. "We met with Jody and her daughter Lindsay, and we talked to the police. It turns out Jay was wearing the right color shirt and was in the right place."

"You know, I've been doing some research on Jay myself," Tess said. She pushed herself back and looked up. There was a look LuAnn couldn't read on her face.

"Did you find anything?" Janice asked.

"No." Tess leaned back in the chair and cocked her head. "That's what's really strange. There's nothing."

"What do you mean?" LuAnn stepped forward to try to see Tess's computer screen.

"I mean, yeah, there's some basic information. Stuff you would expect. Pictures from golf tournaments, the country club, normal stuff like that."

LuAnn laughed. "Golf tournaments and the country club are hardly normal things to most people."

"But given who is on this tour and how much it costs to be here, it makes sense," Tess said. "So I started thinking about what else we know about him."

"We know he's not from Ohio, even though he says he is," Janice said.

"Probably true, but difficult to prove," Tess said. "But his wife did mention that he'd been in the army, so I decided to try to see if I could find out whether that was true or not."

LuAnn wanted to ask who in the world would lie about something like that, but she stopped herself. Who would lie about any of it? But she was nearly certain he had.

"I saw something on the news about how many people pretend to be veterans," Janice said.

"What?" LuAnn hadn't seen it and was dismayed. "Is that something people really do?"

"Sadly, I'm afraid it is," Tess said. "There was even a book about people who claim to be Vietnam veterans and how most people—including most employers and reporters—simply believe them without checking into their stories."

"That's awful," LuAnn said. "The men and women who fight for this country deserve every bit of respect and honor they get, and it's just wrong to pretend you're a veteran when you haven't earned that right."

"I totally agree," Tess said. "Which is why I wanted to look into it."

"What did you find?" LuAnn asked.

"Were you able to find his military records online?" Janice asked, leaning in to get a better look at the screen.

"No, sadly, I couldn't do that." Tess shook her head. "I did try, but you can request them online only if you're the veteran or next of kin."

"That's probably a good thing," LuAnn said. The nation's veterans deserved their privacy.

"It is, but it doesn't make my task easy," Tess said. "But I found out that military records are available to search at the National Archive in Washington DC, and there's a military personnel records center in St. Louis where anyone can request personnel records."

"Too bad we don't live in St. Louis," LuAnn said. It was an eight-hour drive. Too far for a quick jaunt to check out the archive.

"That's what I thought," Tess said.

LuAnn watched her, waiting for her to go on. There was a "but" coming, she was sure.

"But I decided to give them a call. Just to see, you know?"

"Did they tell you anything?" Janice asked.

"They were very friendly and helpful. Just really great people."

"But what did they tell you?" LuAnn leaned forward.

"Well, they couldn't give me any specific information about Jay. To do that, I'd have to come in and submit a paper form, or I could mail it in, but it would take weeks to get a response."

"And?" Was Tess drawing this out on purpose?

"They could confirm that there was indeed a record for a Jay Aaron Carroll."

LuAnn let out a pent-up breath. She didn't know if she was glad to find out that was true or not. "Okay, so we know that, at least, was true."

"I sweet-talked the man on the phone a bit, and he told me that Jay enlisted in the army in January 1969." Tess was obviously pleased with herself. And, LuAnn had to admit, it was pretty impressive.

"How did you manage that?" Janice asked.

"His name was Wyman, and so I told him that was my grandpa's name, which is true, and soon we just got to chatting. I may have mentioned that my husband passed away recently, and, I don't know, I think he took pity on me."

"Did you tell him why you were interested in Jay?" Janice asked.

"Not exactly. He probably thought I was looking into family history, and I didn't correct him. But everything I said was true."

"Did he tell you when Jay left the army?" LuAnn asked.

"No, sadly, I couldn't get him to share that, or why he left the army. But at least we know that much of his story is true."

LuAnn nodded, thinking. "If only there was some way to find out how much of the rest of it is true," she said.

"I thought about that," Tess said. "I also looked into trying to get ahold of his vital records online. Birth certificate, marriage certificate, that sort of thing, There are lots of genealogy sites that promise access to all sorts of records, and maybe they really do. But they're very expensive, and I have my doubts."

LuAnn thought for a moment. It might be worth it, if it gave them answers.

"There's another way to find out the same information, though," Tess said.

"How?" Janice and LuAnn asked at once.

"Jay told you he was born outside Columbus, right?" Tess said. "So I was wondering if you wanted to take a little trip with me this afternoon."

"To Columbus? That would have to be a whirlwind day trip."

"Exactly." Tess smiled. "I found a little photography store that sells disposable cameras and props for the selfie station for the wedding, so I need to go anyway. I was wondering if you'd be interested in making a stop by the vital records office too."

"When?" LuAnn checked her watch. It was just past noon now. It was a two-hour drive to Columbus. She was supposed to meet Brad at the florist tonight, but if they hurried, she could just make it.

Tess shrugged. "If we leave now, we could make it to the vital records office and then to the photo store and be back here for a late supper."

"The rooms are all cleaned," Janice said. "And since there's no one checking in or out today, I can handle things here. And Robin and Taylor will be glad to stay a bit longer, I'm sure."

LuAnn thought for a moment. She had to admit she was intrigued. "Let me just grab something to eat, and I'll be ready to go."

LuAnn wouldn't want to live in a big city like Columbus, but she did enjoy coming to visit. There were people everywhere, walking through the streets and the parks along the riverfront and ducking in and out of shops. There was so much life and excitement here. They found the Franklin County Bureau of Vital Statistics office and made their way inside. There were several desks and a small waiting area, but the office was quiet.

"Can I help you?" a woman called out, gesturing for them to step toward her desk. She was thin and wiry and had short brown hair, and she smiled as they approached.

"Hi there," LuAnn said uncertainly as she stepped forward. "We're interested in finding a birth certificate."

"Sure thing." The woman opened a drawer in her desk and pulled out a sheet of paper. She pushed it across the counter and handed LuAnn a pen. LuAnn looked down at the form. It was an application for a copy of a birth certificate, and she was supposed to fill out the full name, as well as date of birth and place of birth.

"What if I don't have all the information?" she asked.

"Just fill out as much as you can." LuAnn noticed that there was a small brass nameplate that said Amy Nylund on her desk. Amy wore a brown blouse and khaki pants, and a tiger's eye necklace hung around her neck. She was pretty much wearing all brown, LuAnn noted. "Is this for yourself?"

"No." LuAnn wasn't sure how much to say.

"It's for a friend," Tess added. Which was true enough, LuAnn supposed, but she held her breath. She had no idea what the rules were and whether they would even be allowed to look for a birth certificate for someone else.

"That's okay," Amy said, answering LuAnn's unspoken question. "Ohio is an open records state. That means birth records are considered public information, so you can look up birth certificates for anyone you want."

LuAnn tried not to show how relieved she was. She filled out her name and address and entered what she knew of Jay's information: Jay Aaron Carroll, and his birthday, January 21, 1947.

"He said he was born outside Columbus, so I'm assuming that means his birth certificate would be here," LuAnn said.

"Most likely." Amy took the paper and looked it over.

"Is there..." LuAnn didn't quite know how to phrase this bit. "Is there any way he would know we were looking up his records?"

Amy gave her a reassuring smile. "We do keep records of request, but we don't alert people when their records are requested," she said. "If he filed a request, we'd have to let him see who had accessed his records, but it's not like we publicize that or anything. Most likely he'll never find out."

"Oh good." LuAnn felt better about this with every word.

"Should I go see what I can find out?"

A small part of LuAnn was disappointed that they wouldn't get to dig through the old records themselves. She had always loved sifting through historical records, searching for hidden answers in the documents. Some people thought a historian's job was dry and dull, just going through the dusty old papers other people left behind. But LuAnn was fascinated by the remnants of lives that had gone before, trying to understand what the people were like and how they thought and what their stories were.

But Tess answered, "Yes, please," and LuAnn realized it was probably for the best. If they didn't want to be here for hours, it would be better for a professional to do the job. Amy would know just where to look.

"Great. Give me a minute. I'll take this into the back and see what I can find."

Amy walked toward a door in the rear of the room and disappeared into the back.

"Here goes nothing." LuAnn looked at Tess and let out a breath. They both sat in silence for a moment. The room was lit with fluorescent lighting that popped and hissed but did nothing to lessen the grayish gloom. The woman at the station to the left was typing something on her computer.

"It will be fine, no matter what we find out," Tess said. Then, after another moment of quiet, she turned to LuAnn.

"What time are you meeting Brad tonight?"

"Sevenish, after he gets done with a showing. The flower shop is staying open late so we can look at options."

"Nice of them to stay open late."

"I'm sure it doesn't hurt to keep our business. After all, we have quite a few events where we decorate with flowers."

"You're probably right." Tess laughed. "I'm so curious to meet Lauren."

It took LuAnn a moment to catch up with the change in topic, but then she nodded. "I am too," she said. "Brad seems to think she's wonderful, so I'm sure she must be."

"But does she really not care about the details of her wedding?" Tess tilted her head.

LuAnn shrugged. "I guess not. It seems a bit strange, but I don't know. I guess there are things that are more important than the color of the flowers and whatnot."

LuAnn thought back to the time leading up to her almost-wedding. LuAnn was a planner, she had always been one, and planning for this life event put her in her element. She threw herself into research, lists, and details in the months leading up to the big day. Jesse's only request had been that the congregation sing "Blessed Assurance" during the ceremony. It was his favorite hymn. Thinking about it now, LuAnn couldn't help but hum it quietly.

"Are you thinking about Jesse?" Tess asked quietly.

LuAnn nodded. It still stung. All these years later, it still stung.

"He was a good man," Tess said, and put her hand on LuAnn's arm.

LuAnn nodded. Jesse had died of an undiagnosed heart condition two weeks before their wedding. When Jesse's brother had called from the hospital to tell her he'd been taken away in an ambulance, LuAnn had thought it was the cruelest joke she'd ever heard, but it hadn't taken long for her to realize that it was no trick. Jesse had passed away before she made it to the hospital. She'd never even gotten to say good-bye. All of their dreams, all of their hopes…gone, just like that. LuAnn didn't know how she would have survived it if it hadn't been for Tess and Janice. Her two best friends—and the unflagging support of her mother—had gotten her through the worst days of her life. While Tess and Janice held her up, Mother had quietly canceled the caterer and gotten a refund on the hall.

"Does it bring it all back, planning weddings now?" Tess asked.

LuAnn nodded. They had done a few weddings at the inn, including a second wedding for their friend and handyman Tory Thornton and his ex-wife, Beverly, and it wasn't that she minded. Not at all. LuAnn loved planning parties, and there was just something about a wedding to give you hope for the world. LuAnn thought it was beautiful to see two people promising to forsake all others and commit themselves to one another for the rest of their days. It was awe-inspiring to be able to place such trust in another person. But if she was honest, it did some-times make her wonder what her life might have been like if things had worked out differently. Would she have had chil-dren? Would they have stayed in the area? Would she still have been able to travel the world, or had a career of her own? LuAnn knew she would never know the answers to those ques-tions, and she had to trust that the Lord knew what He was doing, that He'd allowed the disappointments and heartache so He could use her in different ways.

"It does bring it all back," LuAnn said. "But mostly in good ways. I remember the excitement and the anticipation that I felt, the sense of wishing that time would speed up because I just didn't want to wait anymore." She touched the silver bracelet she wore. "Maybe it's because I never got to feel the disappointment after the honeymoon wears off, never had to experience the inevitable fights and challenges of marriage, that I remember the happy expectation most of all."

"You *are* very good at relating to the excited brides." Tess smiled. "And at pulling together all the details to make a wedding come together."

LuAnn shrugged. "I really do enjoy it. I don't know. I guess my point is, I can sort of see why Lauren might not feel the need to stress herself out about the perfect shade for the maid of honor dress. Maybe she's just really excited to be marrying the man she loves and letting the rest of it fall to the wayside."

Tess chuckled. LuAnn knew that Tess's wedding had been perfectly planned and held at the church Jeffrey's family had attended for decades. There had been eight bridesmaids, all in matching lavender floor-length gowns, and punch and cake at the golf club afterward. Would she have chosen differently if she had to do it all over? Just as LuAnn was about to ask, Amy came back into the room. She held a few manila folders under her arm, and LuAnn couldn't read the look on her face. She sat up straighter and waited for Amy to sit down. As Amy lowered herself into her chair, LuAnn realized she'd been holding her breath.

"I found the birth certificate," Amy said.

"You did?"

She nodded and pulled a photocopy out of the folder. It was rimmed in swirls, and the blanks had been filled in by typewriter. Jay Aaron Carroll, it said, had been born on January 21, 1947 at Riverside Methodist Hospital in Columbus. His parents were Arlene and Stanley Carroll.

LuAnn looked it over. It all looked normal. She wasn't sure what she'd been expecting, but she felt a strange sense of disappointment.

"Well, that's good," Tess said. "So it all checks out. He is who he says he is."

LuAnn nodded, but she still felt…lost somehow. She hadn't really thought he had been lying. Not exactly. But it still felt…

Amy cleared her throat. LuAnn looked up. There it was. That look on her face. LuAnn waited for her to go on.

"I'm not sure whether you're interested in any other vital records for Jay Carroll or not," she said.

"Sure," LuAnn said. "Did you find a marriage license?"

"No…" she said slowly. "No, not that."

Now that she thought about it, that didn't seem so strange. It seemed likely he and Jacqueline would have gotten married in Kentucky, given how proud Jacqueline was of her family history. So it wasn't a huge surprise there was nothing on record here.

"I did find this though." Amy took another paper out of the folder and pushed it across the table.

"What is this?" Tess's brow wrinkled as she looked down. LuAnn looked at the paper and tried to make sense of what she was seeing.

"Certificate of death?" Tess said.

That was what LuAnn was seeing too. A death certificate for Jay Aaron Carroll. According to this, he'd passed away in 1968.

What in the world?

"But that's impossible," Tess said. "Jay is in Marietta right now. We talked to him this morning."

Amy didn't answer for a minute, and then she shook her head.

"I'm afraid there's really only one explanation," she said. "I don't know who the man you know really is, but it's clear he's not Jay Aaron Carroll."

CHAPTER TEN

"What do you mean he's not Jay Aaron Carroll?" LuAnn said.

Amy shook her head. "I'm afraid I can't tell you much more than that. I don't know who he is. But I can tell you that Jay passed away more than forty years ago."

"But then who is the man at our inn?" Tess asked.

"I don't know," Amy said. "You're sure about the birth date?"

LuAnn nodded and pulled out her phone. First, she took a picture of the death certificate. Then she scrolled until she found the photo of the driver's license and held it out. "Maybe there's more than one person with that name?" she asked.

"Sure, that's possible," Amy said. She shifted in her chair, and it squeaked under her. "But with that birth date? Born in Franklin County? This is the only record, I'm afraid."

"There has to be a mistake," Tess said.

"Okay..." LuAnn tried to wrap her head around this. "So what happened? How did the man at our inn end up with a driver's license in the name of someone who is long dead?"

"I don't really know," Amy said. "I mean, I guess it's possible that the man you know as Jay adopted the identity of the original Jay. The most obvious reason would be that he needed a Social Security number and took this person's."

Was that possible? Had Jay—their Jay—been born under a different name but adopted the dead man's name and Social Security number? But how? And for what reason?

"But how would that work?" Tess asked. "Aren't there agencies that monitor that kind of thing?"

Amy smiled. "Well, yes, I suppose that's our job. But our agency wasn't nearly as large back then, and it's likely that no one ever really looked, especially if, say, he registered for a marriage license in a different state. I mean, now that these things are computerized, it's easier, but assuming he got married quite a while ago, they wouldn't necessarily have gone back and checked another state's records to make sure the man applying for the marriage license was alive."

LuAnn saw her point. But it still seemed impossible. "You're saying that our guest stole someone else's identity?" She'd thought this kind of thing only happened today, when someone made the mistake of handing out their Social Security number or bank account number to scammers.

"I'm not saying that necessarily," Amy said. "I don't know what really happened here. All I'm saying for sure is that our records show that the man who was born Jay Aaron Carroll passed away many years ago."

LuAnn leaned back in her chair.

"But…the man at our inn. Who is he?"

None of them knew how to answer.

They talked over the various possibilities as they drove to the photo shop. Maybe Tess had misunderstood when Jay told them where he'd been born. Maybe his birthday was wrong on his driver's license. That happened, LuAnn thought. She'd once known someone who'd had to correct a similar mistake. Maybe there really were two babies born with that name in Franklin County on that day, and Amy had only pulled the file for one of them. Maybe it had all been a terrible mistake somehow.

But the more they talked it through, the less convinced LuAnn became. She'd known something was off about Jay from the beginning. The way he'd reacted to her had set off alarm bells, and now they had proof that something was funny.

They arrived at the photo shop, and while Tess loaded up a basket with disposable cameras and props for a photo booth, they continued to discuss the situation, but they didn't come up with any new possibilities. By the time they got back in the car, LuAnn was pretty sure there was only really one possibility.

"He's lying about his identity."

"But who is he, really?" Tess asked.

"And why would he take on someone else's life?" LuAnn asked. Did Jacqueline know? Had he been fooling people for decades?

"I don't know," Tess said. "But I know one thing for sure. We're going to find out."

CHAPTER ELEVEN

October 3, 1859

By the time Prudence walked to the post office in town, Baby Moses strapped snug to her chest, her skirts were muddy, and she was chilled. Jason had needed the horses this afternoon, but Prudence did not want to wait.

She stepped inside the small building, marched straight to the counter, and asked for a stamp. The return address in the corner of the envelope bore the name Effie Collins. The girl Prudence had been once upon a time. Then, tentatively, gently, she put her letter in the box, saying a prayer that it would find its way to her aunt somehow, and then she turned to start the long walk back to the farm.

It would be weeks before she heard anything back, she reminded herself. If she ever heard anything at all.

But still. She couldn't help feeling that she would finally have news of her family soon.

They were almost back to Marietta when LuAnn's cell phone rang. She dug it out of her purse. It was a Marietta number, and she answered it cautiously.

"Is this LuAnn Sherrill?"

"Yes, this is LuAnn."

"Ms. Sherrill. This is Officer Lewis from the police station."

"Oh. Hello, Randy." LuAnn turned to Tess, in the driver's seat, and whispered, "It's the police." She put the phone on Speaker so Tess could listen.

Tess nodded and kept her eyes on the road.

"We believe we have your wallet."

"What?" LuAnn couldn't believe it. "Really?"

"It was found in the Dumpster behind McHappy's." That was the beloved donut shop in town. "If you're available to come by the police station, you can pick it up anytime."

"Uh." She glanced at Tess.

Tess mouthed, "We'll go now."

"I'll be there shortly. Thank you."

"They found it!" Tess exclaimed as soon as LuAnn ended the call. She had exited the highway and was passing the athletic fields for Marietta College. The police station was only a few blocks away, on Putnam Street.

Soon, they were heading up the steps and into the police station. They were quickly ushered inside and seated in Chief Mayfield's office again.

"Well, now, this is special. Twice in one day," the police chief joked. "If only the kitchen at the barbecue place had taken their trash out a bit sooner, I could have saved you a second trip."

"So it was found when they took out the trash?" LuAnn asked.

"Exactly." Chief Mayfield nodded. "We were told the kid working there took out the garbage and noticed it on top of the pile of bags just before he tossed the new ones in." He reached into his desk drawer and pulled out a plastic storage bag. The wallet was inside. "Judging from the condition, I think it's safe to assume it had been there for a while."

He handed the bag to LuAnn, and she took it. A smear of chocolate icing just about covered the front side of the wallet, and there were patches of fine black powder in several places.

"I'm sorry about the powder. It's nearly impossible to lift fingerprints from leather, but we tried."

LuAnn turned the bag over. The back of the wallet was in about the same condition as the front. The wallet was stuffed, though. She'd imagined it would be flat and floppy, but it seemed like some of her things might still be inside.

"Did the fingerprints help?" Tess asked.

"I'm afraid we didn't get much. Forensics is working on it, but it's unlikely there's anything we can use."

LuAnn opened the bag and was hit by the smell of barbecue sauce.

"Extra tangy, I see," Tess joked.

LuAnn reached in and pulled out her wallet. It was greasy, and the stains might never come out of the leather, but when she opened it up, there was her driver's license and her credit and insurance cards. The cash was gone, but everything else seemed to be there.

"Oh, thank goodness." The wallet may be ruined, but at least she wouldn't have to make a trip to the DMV or order new insurance cards.

"But how did it end up in the Dumpster?" Tess asked.

"We're still working on that," Chief Mayfield said. "But we're getting closer."

"Does that mean the security camera footage from the museum showed something?" LuAnn asked.

"It means we're getting closer," Chief Mayfield repeated.

He wouldn't tell her then. Well, as long as they found the guy, it didn't matter.

LuAnn thanked the police chief, and then she and Tess returned home. The tour group was out to dinner, and the inn was quiet. LuAnn was grateful for the peace. She had more questions for Jay than ever before, but she wasn't quite ready to formulate them yet. They found Janice in the fourth-floor kitchen, stirring something in a pot on the stove.

"Hi there," she called. "How did it go?"

"It was . . ." LuAnn wasn't sure what to say. "Informative."

"LuAnn got her wallet back," Tess volunteered. It was hardly the most important thing that had happened, but it was the easiest to explain, and LuAnn was grateful she'd started there.

"Really?" Janice moved away from the stove and picked up a knife. "Where was it?" LuAnn stepped closer and saw that she was slivering fresh basil. There were tomato seeds and the skin of an onion on a cutting board. Janice was making fresh marinara sauce. LuAnn's stomach grumbled. The sunlight was starting to fade from the sky and it was well past their normal dinnertime. She didn't know if she'd have time for a bite before she had to leave to meet Brad.

They explained how the wallet had been found behind the donut shop, and Janice listened as she carefully sliced the leaves.

"They don't know who took it yet," Tess said. "But at least she got it back."

"Huh." Janice picked up the cutting board she was using and used the knife to scrape the basil into the sauce. "I actually think I may be able to help you there."

LuAnn had to have heard her wrong. "What do you mean?"

"Well, keep in mind you guys have been gone a long time," Janice said. She had a knowing smile on her face.

"Okay." LuAnn waited for her to go on. It was true, it had been just under six hours. But what did that have to do with anything?

"When the group came back to the inn to rest after lunch, I naturally went downstairs to make sure everyone was doing okay."

"Naturally." Tess grinned. "And let me guess. You checked on one guest in particular?"

"Well, I had to make sure Jay had enjoyed the museum," Janice said.

"And?"

"And he enjoyed it very much. His wife loved it even more."

LuAnn waited for her to get to the point. She definitely had one, LuAnn could see by the smile. She was pleased about something.

"I didn't learn much from talking to Jay and Jacqueline, to be honest," she said. "His favorite part of the museum was the towboat." That was an authentic sternwheeler tied in the river, LuAnn knew. "Jacqueline liked the gift shop, and she bought Christmas ornaments for their grandchildren. I couldn't work out from talking to them whether either of them was around when the wallet was taken. But I did talk with Meaghan, and she told me that the group stuck together inside the museum, so Jay was with the rest of the group during the tour."

Janice stirred the pot, and tiny wisps of steam rose off the surface. LuAnn noticed that a pot of water was heating on the back burner.

"She didn't know whether he went to the gift shop or not," Janice continued. "She said she was waiting outside, so she didn't see anything."

"So there's no way to know whether Jay took the wallet at the museum or not," Tess said.

"I didn't say that," Janice said. "I just said Meaghan didn't know."

Tess cocked her head, and Janice gave a small smile. "I got a call from Jody," she said. "They got ahold of the security camera footage and asked if I wanted to take a look."

"You saw it?" LuAnn asked. "What did it show?"

"Come see." She set the wooden spoon down and turned down the burner, and then she moved toward the sitting area, where her laptop was resting on the coffee table. They all piled onto the couch, and LuAnn noticed a thumb drive in the side of the laptop. That was how Jody had made a copy of the footage then. The screen showed a grainy black-and-white image of the lobby and the open doorway to the gift shop. Janice moved the bar at the bottom of the screen left to return to the start of the footage. The time stamp in the corner said 10:37. The camera angle was from above, meaning the camera must have been placed on the ceiling across the lobby.

"Here's where you can see Lindsay park the stroller just outside the gift shop," Janice said, and LuAnn watched as, on screen, she did exactly that. Jody and Lindsay appeared on the screen, and they could see Lindsay scan the area, decide the stroller was much too large to navigate the narrow aisles of the gift shop, and park the stroller just outside the wide doorway opening. Jody was right. Strollers were getting bigger by the day. There was a bag strapped to the handlebars, which LuAnn assumed must be the diaper bag, as well as a cup holder and a bin underneath the seat piled with toys and other unidentifiable baby things.

On screen, Lindsay bent down to unstrap Carter. She hoisted him out of the stroller, and then she and Jody went into the gift shop, leaving the stroller—and the open diaper bag—unattended.

"The tour group has already finished their tour, and you can see some of them in the shop." Janice pointed to Mona looking at postcards and Marian looking at the selection of books. "Now you can see Lindsay browsing off over here. And here comes Jacqueline." She used her finger to trace the woman's appearance on screen. She had emerged from a part of the shop that wasn't visible on the screen.

"What's back there?" Tess asked, pointing to where she had come from.

"I don't know. More stuff to buy, I guess." Janice shrugged. "It doesn't really matter though, because look." She pointed to the right-hand corner of the screen, where Jay appeared, coming into the shop and marching over to Jacqueline. He said something to her, and she nodded, and then Jay went back off to the right and disappeared from the shot.

"He doesn't appear again," Janice said. LuAnn wondered how many times she'd watched this footage while they were gone.

"But look over here." She used the bar to move the footage forward, and then slowed it down when a man appeared to the left of the screen, wearing a white polo shirt and a straw fedora hat.

"That's him." LuAnn knew instantly. The hat blocked his face, at least from this angle, and she couldn't spot anything identifying about his clothing. But something about the way he moved registered on a subconscious level, and she recognized him instantly. "That's the guy who took my wallet."

"Watch what he does," Janice said. Very casually, the man walked over toward the stroller, spotted the diaper bag, and reached in. It was so quick they wouldn't have seen it unless they were looking for it. Then he vanished off the right side of the screen.

"Wow. That was smooth," Tess said.

"It's super-quick," Janice says. "He's obviously done this before."

"Yeah, like yesterday for starters," LuAnn said wryly.

"It goes on, but he doesn't appear on the screen again," Janice said.

LuAnn tried to replay the footage in her mind. "Can we see it again?"

Janice used the bar to scroll to the left and replayed the footage. LuAnn watched as the scene played out again.

"There isn't really any way to tell much about the thief," Janice said. "Unfortunately."

"But it's clear that it's not Jay," Tess said.

Janice nodded. "Which, I mean, I guess that's great."

LuAnn wanted to laugh. Janice was clearly disappointed that her theory had been wrong, but she was also wrestling with the relief that they didn't have a thief under their roof.

"It's very good," LuAnn said. "It doesn't get us any closer to finding out who took the wallet, but it's nice to know it's not Jay."

And, she realized, on some level she'd already known as much. Something about Jay's reaction to her seemed to go much deeper than a wallet, and all along she'd had the sense that there was something bigger at play here.

"But we still don't know why he reacted the way he did when he saw LuAnn," Tess said, voicing exactly what LuAnn was thinking. "If it wasn't that he recognized her from her driver's license, what was it?"

"I don't know." Janice shook her head. "My theory has been shot to pieces," she said. "So I don't have a clue."

LuAnn was thinking through every interaction with Jay in the past couple of days, trying to make sense of it. His accent. The pale, haunted look he'd gotten when she'd met him. His insistence that they'd never met, when something inside her told her a different story. And then, what they'd learned this afternoon added a whole new layer.

"We need to find out who he really is," LuAnn said.

Janice looked at her. "What do you mean?"

"Wait till you hear this," Tess said, and told her what they had learned at the Vital Records Office.

"So you mean he's not really Jay Carroll?" Janice asked.

"Jay Carroll died in 1968."

"But maybe there were two of them? Two men with the exact same name? Born in the same city on the same day?"

"Even if that were a possibility, the records clerk would have been able to pull up two sets of documents," LuAnn said. "But she only found one."

"But that doesn't make sense," Janice said.

"I've been thinking about it," Tess said, "and I think it's pretty clear that whoever Jay was before, he needed a new identity, and he took the identity of a man who'd recently died as his own."

LuAnn had to admit it made the most sense of any theory so far. "But how does that work?"

"You got me," Tess said. "We'd have to do some research to find that out."

"But the bigger question is why," Janice said. "Why would he change his identity and take on the identity of another man?" She was quiet for a moment, and then, under her breath, she asked, "Do you think he's a criminal?"

"I guess it's possible," LuAnn said. "Maybe he escaped from prison and changed his name to avoid being found? Or maybe he changed it so he wouldn't be found and arrested in the first place?"

"Or maybe he's in the witness protection program," Tess said, looking at LuAnn. "Like your father. He needed a new identity so bad guys couldn't find him."

"Maybe." This seemed less likely to LuAnn. For one thing, for all its appearances in movies and books, the number of people actually involved in the government program was quite small. LuAnn had already encountered a couple of them in her life, and it seemed unlikely she would meet more. But beyond that, this didn't add up. "I think they usually create a new identity for you, not take the identity of someone who died."

"Well, there has to be a logical reason that he took someone's identity," Tess said.

LuAnn nodded. "But I have no clue what that reason is," she said. Or, she added to herself, what it was about him that seemed so deeply familiar to her.

CHAPTER TWELVE

A little while later, LuAnn met Brad at Blooms, a lovely florist shop on Front Street. LuAnn had called the owner, Katrina Kingston, yesterday, and Katrina was glad to stay open a little late so she could help LuAnn and Brad select flowers for Lauren's wedding. LuAnn saw Brad standing in front of the shop as she walked down the street, and she couldn't help the little flutter that went through her. He really was a handsome man.

Brad turned and saw her, and she didn't think she was imagining the way his face changed. It wasn't just that he smiled. His eyes suddenly seemed more alive.

"You look lovely," he said, leaning in to give her a hug. "Shall we?" He opened the door, and she stepped in and was greeted by the sweet scent of roses and lilies.

"It smells wonderful in here," LuAnn said, taking in a deep breath.

"Thank you," Katrina said, coming out of an office at the back of the small shop. "I really do have the best job in the world. I get to smell it all day." Katrina was tall and wore her brown hair in a long braid. She couldn't be more than thirty-five, LuAnn thought, but she had a confident air that made her seem more mature.

"So. You're looking for flowers for a wedding, right?" Katrina walked around the counter and stood next to them in the middle of the room. The original hardwood floors in the old building had been refinished and creaked under their feet, which LuAnn found charming. The walls were painted a deep grayish blue that really worked with the big plate-glass window at the front of the shop.

"That's right. Brad's goddaughter is getting married on Saturday, and we're tasked with picking out the flowers." LuAnn took in the coolers with premade baskets and bouquets along the back and bins of fresh flowers along one wall. Roses and lilies and freesia and iris were mixed with aster, delphinium, amaryllis, and heather. It was intoxicating.

"Are you looking for flowers for the wedding party or the reception or both?"

"Both, I suppose," Brad said. "Though the wedding party is small. The bride has a maid of honor, and the groom will have his brother stand with him. So there's not much to do there."

"The reception is at the inn?"

"It will be outdoors, in the yard, assuming the weather holds," LuAnn said. "We'll have white tablecloths and napkins and simple chairs. So nothing too formal."

"And what about decorations for the church? Flowers for the altar or the ends of the pews?"

LuAnn looked at Brad and shook her head. "No, I don't think so." Christ Fellowship Church was lovely just as it was. They didn't need to dress it up.

"Great. And did you have any thoughts about what kind of flowers you're looking for?"

"We want to keep it pretty simple," Brad said. "I don't think anything exotic is really her style." He gestured at a basket that prominently featured bird of paradise.

"That's good, since it would be tricky to get enough of the more specialty-type flowers on such short notice." Katrina wandered over to the bins and selected a blush-colored peony. "I love peonies for a bridal bouquet. Maybe in different shades of pink and white?"

"That would be nice," LuAnn said.

"And then for the tables, maybe we could keep it simple. Maybe we mix some white peonies with daisies and these gorgeous dahlias?" She pulled a light pink flower from the bin and held it up. "Maybe add in a bit of fresh greenery for color. We'll keep the centerpieces low, so they're not intrusive, and we can do simple glass bowls."

"That sounds lovely," LuAnn said. She looked at Brad to see his reaction.

"If you think that sounds good, it sounds good to me." Brad was looking around, taking it all in, but seemed to be out of his element.

"Well, that was easy." Katrina laughed. "Now, how many do you think you'll need?"

LuAnn and Katrina discussed delivery and pricing. Brad put down a deposit, and then they were stepping out of the shop.

"That was relatively painless," Brad said. "How about some pizza to celebrate?" Over the Moon Pizza was just down the street.

"I'm happy to join you for pizza," LuAnn said. She'd only had a few bites of the pasta Janice had made before she had to run out to meet Brad. "But did you think looking at flowers would be painful?"

"I don't know." He started walking down Front Street. "I've never really had to think about flowers before. Stephanie handled all that for our wedding. I just showed up and put on the boutonniere I was handed."

"I'm sure you did more than that."

"Oh, yeah, I mean, I cared about the cake, for sure. I must have taste-tested a dozen flavors to make sure we picked the best one. But flowers?" He laughed. "I'm afraid I had nothing to do with that piece of it."

"Did you get married here in town?" LuAnn had never heard about his wedding before, or really much about his relationship with his late wife at all, and she was curious.

"We did. In the big Presbyterian church on Fourth. Her family has been members there for generations."

LuAnn knew the large stone building. It was beautiful, but imposing. "That's a lovely place."

"It really is."

"Is that when you bought the house you live in now?" LuAnn had been to Brad's house, a cute and well-maintained bungalow, a few times.

"No, we rented for a few years. A little apartment over on Warren Street." He laughed. "It was kind of a dump, looking back on it now, but we didn't care. We were just happy it was ours."

"What was Stephanie like?" LuAnn worried she might have crossed the line with that question, but Brad didn't seem to mind.

"She was...Maybe passionate isn't the right word, but she was the kind of person who got an idea and threw herself into it completely. So she was completely dedicated to teaching and to decorating our home and to whatever cause she was championing at the moment—and there were a lot of them." He rubbed his chin. "She loved to laugh, but she also had dark moods that could be difficult."

LuAnn hated that she felt a small measure of comfort at this. Stephanie hadn't been perfect then. Somehow, she wasn't sorry to hear it.

They had reached the pizza place and were seated at a table at the back, where LuAnn kept the conversation going.

"You two never had kids?"

"We wanted to. We tried for years, really. But it just never happened. We went to all kinds of doctors, but no one could ever figure out what was going on." He unfolded his napkin and placed it on his lap. "I figured it was God's way of redirecting our energies elsewhere and tried to trust that He had other things in store for us. And Stephanie tried to accept it, she really did. But she never quite got over the disappointment. She wanted a baby so badly."

"That must have been so hard." LuAnn wasn't sure what else to say. She had wanted children too, though in the end she'd never had the opportunity. Instead, she'd traveled and thrown herself into teaching, but she had never had to face the kind of heartache and disappointment that must have come from trying to get pregnant and being let down, month after month.

"It was really tough on her. And it was hard on our marriage, honestly. I probably wasn't as sensitive or kind as I could have been. I worked hard on building my business. That was my way of coping. But I think in many ways she felt like she was going through it alone, which was really difficult for her."

"I'm so sorry." LuAnn tucked her napkin into her lap as a waitress placed menus in front of them. "Did you ever consider adopting?"

"We did consider it. We even put ourselves on a waiting list for a while. But we stalled for years, and then once we decided to go for it, by the time there was a potential match, we weren't sure we were still up for it."

"It's a huge commitment, raising a child. You'd have to be certain."

"It is. And we had full lives without one. But I don't know. Like I said, Steph never quite got over the disappointment. Honestly, that's kind of why Lauren has always been so special to us. In the midst of this dark period, Mark found out his wife was expecting and asked us to be the godparents to his baby, and that was such a gift. Lauren was just what we needed. We adored her from the day she was born."

LuAnn didn't know how to phrase this, so she just asked, "Is it different than it was with your nieces?"

"Oh, very much so. I mean, I didn't even know about Wendy until a year ago." Brad's brother Grant had recently discovered he had another daughter. "And Saffron...well, she's great. But she mostly grew up far away from here, and her mom always kept her and her brother away from our family as much as possible. I don't know. It just wasn't the same. But we were always very involved in Lauren's life, and in many ways she's like the daughter we never had. Here." He pulled out his phone and opened his photos app. "I was looking through some old photos this week. Here's one of her when she was a baby."

Brad held out his phone, and she saw a much-younger Brad sitting on the couch holding a bundle that she supposed was an infant, a big smile on his face. His hair was thicker, and he was a bit thinner, but otherwise it was unmistakably him. And though she knew she was supposed to be admiring the baby in the photo, it was really the woman sitting pressed up against Brad she was most interested in. This must be Stephanie then. She had dark hair that cascaded around her shoulders, and she had high cheekbones and eyes that laughed even in a photograph. She was beautiful. LuAnn felt a pang of disappointment.

"And here's one from Lauren's fourth birthday." The bundle had transformed into a smiling little girl with curly brown hair and a huge smile. She was leaning over a cake with four burning candles.

"She was adorable."

"She really was." Brad laughed. "Sometimes Steph and I would take her out for a day, to the zoo or the Ice Capades or whatever, to give her parents a break. She was so fun to be around, even then. Just enthusiastic about everything." He scrolled to the right, showing LuAnn photos of a dance recital and a prom and Lauren's high school graduation with her whole family, including Brad and Stephanie, gathered around her, and one of her college graduation, standing next to a young man in matching cap and gown.

"That's Ethan." Brad said.

"He's quite handsome."

Brad cleared his throat.

"It makes sense that you're so involved in the wedding, seeing how involved you were in her life," LuAnn said.

He paused for a moment. And then, "I want her to have the best, you know?"

There was something guarded in his words, but he was smiling. LuAnn wondered if his hesitation had to do with Lauren's fiancé.

"When did you first meet Ethan?" she asked.

There it was again. A look that passed over his face. A look that said more than his words did.

"Just a few months ago. She invited me to dinner to meet him." He shrugged. "It was fine. He was all right."

"But..."

Brad didn't say anything for a moment. Then, carefully, "But he doesn't seem to have much ambition."

"He went to college, and he's joining the army. That's often the start of an illustrious career."

"Now he is. But the whole time Lauren was in graduate school working on her nursing degree, he was living at home, making an 'independent film.'" Brad used air quotes around the last two words.

LuAnn didn't see what was so wrong with a young man taking some time to pursue his passion, as long as he had a family who supported it. Especially if the military was on the horizon. But she knew better than to say so.

"Well, he seems to be on a path forward now," she finally said. "And if Lauren has chosen him, there must be something pretty great about him."

Brad made a noise at the back of his throat, somewhere between a cough and a laugh, and then he picked up his menu. "Let's hope so."

"Well, in any case, her wedding is going to be lovely."

He lowered his menu and met her eyes. "Yes, I really do think it will be." And then he added, "And I have you to thank for that."

LuAnn's stomach warmed, and she ducked her eyes before her cheeks turned red. She'd do everything she could to make sure this wedding was beautiful for Lauren—and for Brad.

LuAnn had just locked the front door and was giving the first floor one last look before she headed upstairs when she heard footsteps on the stairs. She looked up and saw Jay coming down.

"Milk?" she asked.

"Yes, thank you," he said.

"Of course." Luann gestured for him to follow her into the café.

"Did you have a nice evening?" she asked. What she really wanted to ask was who he really was, who he had been, and why he was living someone else's life, but she couldn't just come out and ask, so she started here.

"Oh, yes," Jay said. "We went to Austyn's. The restaurant was very nice, and the food was good. Then we went for a walk along the river."

"That's wonderful." LuAnn held up a finger to ask him to wait, and then she hurried into the kitchen and poured a glass of milk. When she came back out, he took the glass and turned to go.

"Have you ever spent time in West Virginia?" LuAnn asked.

He turned back around, his brow wrinkled. "I've been through it a couple times on the way to the East Coast to see our daughter. She lived in Virginia for a while. But I can't say I've spent any real time there." He tilted his head. "Why?"

"You seem so familiar to me," she said, shaking her head. And then she added, "And I can't help but feel like you've got a lot of stories." She couldn't just come out and accuse their guest of identity theft, could she? That was the closest she could get to what she really wanted to say.

For a second—just a tiny fraction of a second, really—he froze, and LuAnn saw that she'd gotten to him. In that moment, she cracked through the shell he'd built around himself. His mouth dropped open, and something like fear flashed in his eyes. But then, just as quickly, it passed, and he let out a laugh. It came out forced.

"That I do," he said. He hesitated, like he wanted to ask her something, but then he simply said, "But I'm afraid I can't share them tonight. I'm beat, and Jacqueline is waiting for me." He turned and started for the stairs.

"Thanks for the milk, Lulu," he called.

Now LuAnn froze. Lulu? That had been her nickname when she was a child, but no one had called her that in a long time.

"What did you call me?"

Jay stood still for a moment. She couldn't see his face, but she saw his shoulders rise just a bit, tensing up, before he finally turned around.

"Surely people must call you that, right?" he said, shrugging. He had put on that jovial voice again, but he was trying just a bit too hard.

He'd slipped up. She saw that clearly now. He did know her; he'd known her when she was a girl. He hadn't meant to reveal that fact, but it had slipped out.

"It's an obvious nickname for LuAnn."

Even if he was right in some ways—it was the most obvious nickname—it didn't change the fact that they hardly had the kind of relationship where they gave each other nicknames.

Without another word, he turned back around and headed up the stairs. LuAnn watched him go, more determined than ever to find out who Jay Aaron Carroll really was.

CHAPTER THIRTEEN

Wednesday dawned bright and clear, and LuAnn could feel it was going to be hot before she even climbed out of bed. They'd had central air installed when they renovated the inn, but the air still had that heavy feel that promised another sultry day. She hoped it would cool off before Saturday, or the wedding guests were going to roast outside.

But she couldn't worry about that now. This morning she wanted to be up early. She was determined to get Jay to confess how he knew her, so she hurried downstairs and found Winnie already working in the kitchen.

"Good morning, Winnie," LuAnn called. Winnie was stirring batter with a wooden spoon and had the waffle iron out. The coffee was already brewing, filling the air with the rich, earthy scent. LuAnn poured a cup.

"Good morning," Winnie said and set the spoon down. She used the edge of her apron to wipe beads of sweat from her forehead. "I figured waffles would be good so we don't have to turn on the oven."

"That sounds perfect on a morning like this," LuAnn said. She moved to the fridge and pulled out a container of strawberries, a cantaloupe, and a pint of blueberries and started working on a fruit salad. It wasn't long before they heard footsteps on the stairs, and LuAnn went out to the café area to find Meaghan helping herself to a cup of coffee.

"Good morning," LuAnn called.

"Hello there," Meaghan said. She made a face as she closed the spigot and set her coffee cup down. "This stuff is a lifesaver."

"Tell me about it." LuAnn topped off her own cup, and then Meaghan indicated for her to come over. LuAnn saw that she'd already set her ever-present clipboard on one of the tables.

"I wanted to make sure we were still on to tour the basement this afternoon," Meaghan said.

"Of course. We're looking forward to it." For safety reasons, they normally kept guests out of the basement and away from the Underground Railroad tunnel that ran beneath the inn, but the building's history was a big part of the reason Thatch had booked the inn for the guests. She and Tess and Janice had agreed that they would be willing to do a special tour for the group as long as they were all there to supervise.

"Oh, good." Meaghan checked something off on her clipboard. "We're doing the Mound Cemetery this morning. And then the Ghost Tour is tomorrow afternoon."

"You're doing the Ghost Tour?" LuAnn held back a smile. There were several places in Marietta that were rumored to be haunted, including the Castle historic home, the LaBella Hotel, the Gallery, the Hackett Hotel, and the Lafayette Hotel. She supposed that was probably true of any historic property, especially in a town that had once been an outpost on the

western frontier. But LuAnn didn't believe in ghosts, and nei-
ther did the other Inn Crowd ladies, and despite inquiries
from the company that ran the lucrative local business leading
tourists around old basements, the three of them had always
insisted there weren't any ghosts at Wayfarers Inn.

"Those things are always crowd pleasers," Meaghan said,
shrugging. "I don't know what it is. I don't think most people
take it very seriously, they just like to see the old buildings.
But there's something fun about haunted hotels and homes."
She took a sip. "You don't have any ghosts here? Or unexplained phenomena of any kind? No one who died in the
building and comes back to show herself to unwitting guests?"

"We do not," LuAnn said. Well, there had been several
times when a door mysteriously shut or a light somehow turned
on, and Tess liked to joke that a ghost had done it, but they
didn't take it seriously. Yes, there were people who had died in
the building over the nearly two centuries it had stood. LuAnn
did not believe that souls were trapped between worlds or any
of that nonsense. The closest she'd ever come to any of that was
the feeling she sometimes got of being close to Prudence Willard, whose diary had been found in the inn and whose selfless
presence seemed to somehow live on through the decades.

Meaghan looked at her over the rim of her mug. "Too bad.
You could probably make some money off it if you had a
haunted room. Look at how many of the places on this itinerary are hotels."

She held out her clipboard, with the brochure for the ghost
tour on it. LuAnn could see that Meaghan was serious, but she

was smiling as well. Maybe there was a reason so many historic hotels claimed to have ghosts—it stood to reason that with so many people coming and going over the decades that there would be deaths and unexplained phenomena. Or maybe—as Meaghan seemed to be pointing out—rumors of a ghost were just really good for business. Behind her, LuAnn heard the front door open and Taylor's heavy footsteps on the floor.

"Sadly, we'll just have to rely on our beautiful rooms and amazing hospitality," LuAnn said with a smile. She turned and gave Taylor a small wave.

"Don't forget the food. This place is amazing. I stay at a lot of hotels, and these are some of the best breakfasts I've ever had," Meaghan said.

"I'm so glad to hear it. I'll pass your compliments on to Winnie, our cook." LuAnn looked up as Robert and Lisa came down the stairs, this time in matching T-shirts from Yosemite.

"I'm going to take this upstairs and finish getting ready," Meaghan said, holding up her coffee cup. "But I'll be back down in a bit, as soon as those waffles are ready."

She headed back up the stairs and passed Jacqueline, who was on her way down. But where was Jay? After last night's slip-up, LuAnn's plan had been to try to get him alone to ask him some more questions, but he didn't seem to be coming down behind his wife.

"Good morning," LuAnn called out. Did her voice sound a little too cheerful to be natural?

"Hello there." Jacqueline gave her a smile.

"Where's Jay this morning?" LuAnn asked, channeling once again the skills from the acting she'd done in her college years to keep her voice as level and natural as possible.

"He's feeling a little tired, so he wanted to sleep in a bit longer." Jacqueline shrugged. LuAnn tried to ignore the stab of frustration she felt. Was he avoiding her? After what had happened last night, she figured the odds were good. He'd slipped up, and he knew it, and now he didn't want to face her. But how was she going to interrogate him if he wasn't here? "I like sleep as much as the next person," Jacqueline went on, "but there's no way I'm going to skip out on breakfast. Those waffles smell amazing." She stood at the edge of the café and looked at the tables. "I promised I would bring him up some breakfast."

"That's a shame," LuAnn said, and she meant it. Still, she knew she had to make the most of the opportunity. "In that case, would you mind if I join you?"

Jacqueline's eyes lit up. "That would be wonderful. I just hate to eat by myself. Y'all really are the best. This is just the most hospitable inn I've ever stayed at."

LuAnn tried to keep her smile natural as she guided Jacqueline to a table. If only she knew the real reason LuAnn was so anxious to keep her company.

"I'm happy to." She gestured at the coffee urns. "Please help yourself. And Winnie is making the best waffles, so that's what I'm going to have."

"Sounds wonderful. Make that two."

Jacqueline set her purse down on one of the chairs, then walked over and poured herself some coffee. LuAnn gave their order to Taylor. If he was surprised to see her sitting down to eat with a guest, he hid it well and simply smiled as he took their order to the kitchen. When Jacqueline returned, LuAnn took a deep breath and asked, "So, do you and Jay have children?"

She knew they did, but she figured it would be better to start there than to launch into asking Jacqueline why her husband had lied about who he really was. Most people were happy to open up when it came to their children.

"Yes, a boy and a girl." Jacqueline took a sip of her coffee. "Patrick and Mary Grace. Patrick teaches law at the University of Kentucky, so we see him a lot. He's got two kids, both in junior high now. Addison and Liam." She reached down into her purse and pulled out her phone. She unlocked the screen and tapped her photos icon, and then she held out the phone and showed LuAnn. "Addison is twelve now. She just got those braces, and she hates them. She still wants to be a ballerina when she grows up, but we'll see how long that lasts. And Liam is thirteen. He's really into music and plays first trumpet in the school band."

"They're beautiful children."

"I think so." Jacqueline scrolled to another photo. "And Mary Grace was married for a few years. She and her husband recently divorced, but they had one daughter, Evey." She held the phone up again and showed off a picture of a girl with blond curls. LuAnn guessed she was around five.

"She's adorable."

"Thank you." She tucked her phone back into her purse. "How about you? Do you have any children?"

"I'm afraid not," LuAnn said. "I never married." She took a sip of her coffee to keep her voice steady. Normally, talking about Jesse didn't affect her much anymore, but after discussing him with Tess yesterday, the whole thing still felt raw. "I came close once, but it didn't happen."

"Well, there are plenty of other things to do in life," Jacqueline said.

LuAnn nodded. "I've traveled a lot. I loved seeing the world and how differently people live in other places."

"I wish we'd been able to travel more. But Jay always found it hard to get away. He owns an office supply company, and when you own the company, people are relying on you." Jacqueline took another sip of coffee.

"How did you and Jay meet?" *And did he tell you he stole someone else's identity?* she kept herself from adding.

"We met at a wedding. Isn't that always the way?" Jacqueline laughed. "It was one of my good girlfriends, and he was there as a date of one of the groom's cousins. Somehow he managed to see past that hideous pink monstrosity of a bridesmaid dress I was wearing and asked me to dance, and the rest is history."

"His date didn't mind?"

"I don't think she loved it, but I got the sense it wasn't serious. To be honest, the last thing I was thinking of was the date. I was just drawn in by those blue eyes." She laughed again. "I probably should have been more concerned about what's-her-name's feelings, but at the time, I just fell for him, and that was all that mattered to me."

"Was it love at first sight?"

"Something like that. He was so handsome and so kind and such a gentleman. Of course, he'd just gotten out of the army, and I always had a thing about a man in uniform."

"How long did you date before you got married?"

"Four months." She grimaced. "When I think about it now, I realize how lucky we were. I would never advise anyone to marry that quickly. But you couldn't have told me that then. I was in love, and I guess when you know, you know."

"It seems to have worked out," LuAnn said.

"Yes, it did, thankfully. Nearly fifty years later, and here we are. Though it just about killed my parents when we eloped."

"You eloped?"

Jacqueline nodded. "To Atlantic City, of all places. At the time, it seemed so romantic, with the beach and the boardwalk and all that."

That would explain why there wasn't any record of a marriage in Ohio.

"Your parents didn't approve?"

"It wasn't that they didn't approve of Jay. They just didn't know him well, and then, of course, I was their only daughter, so they'd had a big elaborate wedding in mind. Daddy was so mad, and Mother cried for weeks."

"What made you decide to elope?"

"Oh, I don't know." Just then Taylor arrived with two plates of waffles and set them down. "It was Jay's idea, and I guess I just thought it was so romantic. He didn't want to deal with the whole elaborate Southern wedding thing. We knew there would have to be a long engagement, and he said he couldn't wait. What girl wouldn't fall for a man who can't wait to make her his bride?" She unwrapped the silverware Taylor set beside her plate and placed the napkin in her lap. "And, well, we never really said this openly at the time, but Jay wasn't exactly the kind of man my parents had in mind for me, so we didn't exactly want to go the traditional route of getting their approval."

"What do you mean?" LuAnn had gleaned enough to make a guess about what Jacqueline's parents had had in mind for her—a wealthy, well-bred Southern boy—but she wanted to hear what Jacqueline said.

"Oh, you know. He didn't have much money for one," she said. "But he was a hard worker, and I knew he wanted to own a business one day, so I wasn't worried about that." She cut off a small piece of her waffle. "But it was also that he couldn't trace his family history back to the *Mayflower*. You know how these things are. But my parents eventually came around, just like I knew they would. Once they got over the shock, they realized he's a great guy, and they were supportive and welcomed him into the family."

"What about Jay's family? Were they supportive too?"

"Oh." She put the piece of waffle in her mouth and shook her head while she chewed. When she swallowed, she continued, "Jay's family was never around. He had a rough childhood, and he didn't speak to them anymore. Honestly, I've never even met his family."

"Seriously?" LuAnn tried to imagine what this would be like. How could you know someone if you didn't know where they came from and the people who made up their family?

"He doesn't like to talk about it, but I get the sense there was some kind of abuse. I don't know the specifics, because every time I've ever brought it up, he's shut down. Said he doesn't like to go back there, even in his mind. At some point I just stopped asking." She set her fork down and took a sip of her coffee. "But my family is big and warm and welcoming, so we just made him a part of our world. Holidays with my family are the best, anyway. My parents, when they were alive, went over the top at Christmas, and there were always huge meals and mountains of presents. Mother would decorate the whole house. And now my brother's family keeps up the tradition. Jay was overwhelmed the first time he experienced it."

LuAnn tried her best to keep up, but she was still stuck on the main point. "So you've never met anyone in your husband's family?" And Jacqueline somehow didn't think that was a problem, because it meant she didn't have to give up Christmas with her family?

"Oh, I know it must seem strange, but you have to understand, he just doesn't want to talk about it. At all. I tried to for so many years, but, like I said, he would just shut down. Say he worked too hard to escape from there to go back, even in his head. At some point, I had to learn to respect that, no matter how difficult it was. If he can't talk about it, I decided not to ask."

LuAnn nodded, but her mind was racing. Jay's wife had never met a member of his family. Which wasn't really all that surprising if, as they had surmised, he'd adopted the identity of a boy named Jay Aaron Carroll who'd died. Jay would have kept his new wife away from anyone who could have let on that his name was not really Jay. Which meant—LuAnn hated to even think about this possibility—that Jacqueline most likely didn't realize the man she'd been married to for fifty years was a fraud.

"Did you ever try to find out anything about them on your own?"

"No." Jacqueline shook her head. "I thought about it, of course, but I decided that even if I found something, I'd have to keep it a secret from him, and I doubted I'd be able to do that. Better to just let sleeping dogs lie, and all that."

"I'm sure you're right." Then she quickly pivoted. "So that littlest granddaughter of yours. What is she into?"

Jacqueline's face beamed as she talked about Evey's love of horses and her current obsession with unicorns. Grandchildren were always a safe topic, LuAnn thought, and she'd never yet met a grandmother who wasn't willing to talk at length about her grandchildren. But as she listened to Jacqueline go on about dance classes and karate lessons, her brain was working overtime, trying to make sense of what she'd learned. Unless she was a phenomenal actress, Jacqueline had no idea that her husband hadn't been born as Jay. LuAnn already knew, from his enlisting in the army as Jay Carroll, that he took the name before he met Jacqueline. But why? And, underneath it all, the question that was motivating LuAnn to keep digging—who was he, really, and how did she know him?

LuAnn realized she was going to have to find out more about the real Jay Carroll if she had any hope of finding answers.

After the breakfast dishes had been cleaned up and the tour group was on its way to visit the Mound Cemetery, LuAnn grabbed her purse and headed out. Lauren was set to check in today, along with her fiancé and her father, but they didn't expect them to arrive until midafternoon. For now, she was going to visit the library's microfilm archives to see if she could find out anything about the real Jay Carroll. But she'd checked on their website, and they didn't open for another hour, so LuAnn hopped into her car and headed back to the storage unit where her mother's things were stored. When she was there the other day, she'd seen boxes at the back that she'd thought held old photo albums. Her mother had always been meticulous about displaying her photographs in albums—and since she hadn't located them yet, LuAnn guessed they might be there.

She made her way inside the climate-controlled building and went down the hallway on the second floor where her mother's things were. This indoor facility had been more expensive than the outdoor storage units by the highway, but with the humidity and temperature fluctuations around Marietta, LuAnn had been willing to pay more to make sure her mother's things would be protected. She lifted the metal rolling gate and flipped on the little light bulb. To the left, her mother's antique rosewood dresser with the marble top was piled with boxes of old financial records she hadn't sorted through yet. The polished oak rocking chair where her mother had sat to read LuAnn stories and rock her to sleep was upside down on top of a stack of antique quilts. It would take her months to sort through all this stuff, and she'd already cleared out a fair amount. But LuAnn carefully picked her way to the back, where she'd spotted the dusty and battered cardboard boxes that she thought held the old photo albums.

She moved plastic tubs of clothes and bins of books out of the way. Why hadn't she sorted through more of this before she'd dumped it all in here?

But LuAnn knew that she'd been in no state to make decisions about what to keep and what to toss in the dark days after her mother's death. She'd been completely overwhelmed by her grief, and on top of that, she'd recently been reunited with Tess and Janice, and they'd started considering whether to buy the building that became Wayfarers Inn. She hadn't been able to face it then, and coming here, it still somehow felt like no time had passed. The pain of losing her mother was still fresh, especially when she saw her things like this.

LuAnn took a deep breath and tried to focus on the job at hand. She made her way to the back of the unit and moved boxes and bins aside until she freed the dusty cardboard boxes she'd spotted the other day. She opened the top flap on one, and sure enough, she found dozens of photo albums piled inside. LuAnn set the box aside and opened the box underneath it. She lifted the flap and—

Oh my. She sucked in a breath.

Inside the box were about a dozen black plastic circles. LuAnn hadn't seen one of these in years, but she recognized them instantly. They were spools of developed Super-8 film. With them were an old-fashioned projector and a movie camera. LuAnn reached in and lifted the camera out gently. She had wanted this camera so badly. She had picked up babysitting and dog-walking jobs and even taken on a few shifts at the diner, though her mom hadn't encouraged that, to save up enough to buy this.

LuAnn turned the camera over in her hands. She'd had such big dreams back then. She was going to be a movie star and make millions and win Oscars. And she'd known that this camera would be the start.

LuAnn had been so proud when she'd finally saved up enough to buy it. She hadn't factored in how much the film and processing would cost, but eventually she'd saved up enough to buy some of that too, and her mom had picked up the projector at a garage sale. LuAnn shook her head. Money had been so tight. Looking back now, she couldn't believe she'd spent so much on this camera, or that her mom had bought the projector, when the money could have been put to so many other purposes. But LuAnn had set her heart on it, and her mother had always supported her only child's dreams.

LuAnn set the camera down and picked up one of the rolls of film. It was so small and fragile. Was it even still good? Didn't film like this fall apart after so many years? LuAnn wasn't sure, but it would be fun to see what was on the reels after all this time. She vaguely remembered trying to recreate scenes from various movies on her own. She laughed, thinking about it now. She would bring this box too. She hoisted the box and moved it toward the front and then grabbed the box of photo albums as well. She found a cart to wheel the boxes down to her car.

She loaded the boxes, climbed in her car, and checked the time. The library and the archive building would open in just a few minutes. Perfect timing. She drove toward the Marietta Public Library, which was housed in a beautiful brick federal-style building perched on a grassy hill and surrounded by leafy green trees, and then drove past it to the library's satellite building, the local history and genealogy archives on Washington Street. The original oak floors creaked as LuAnn stepped inside the building, and cool, dry air enveloped her.

LuAnn had been here before, and she knew how to load the microfilm into the readers, but she wasn't sure where to start to find what she was looking for.

"You look lost."

LuAnn looked up to find a man in a long-sleeve button-down and glasses watching her. "Do you need some help?"

"I think I probably do." She hoisted her purse up on her shoulder. "I'm actually here to find information about something...a bit strange."

"Ooh. My favorite kind of search." He held out his hand. "I'm Danny."

"LuAnn." LuAnn shook his hand, and he gave her a warm smile. He was probably in his thirties, she guessed, and he had skin the color of nutmeg. "I'm trying to find information about a man named Jay Carroll who died in 1968."

"Is that all?" Danny looked disappointed. "That's not a challenge."

LuAnn laughed. "So where would I start?"

"Do you know where Jay lived?"

"His death certificate was registered in Franklin County." LuAnn reached into her purse, pulled out her phone, and opened up the photo she'd taken of the death certificate. "It looks like he died in Darbydale, Ohio." She walked toward the counter and handed him the phone.

"Oh, wow. You have the actual death certificate there. That makes things easier." Danny looked at the phone and nodded as he read. "Lots of people come in here looking for genealogy research, so I've gotten pretty good at reading these things. Okay, so you know where he was born and where he died, and the cause of death."

"I do?"

Danny enlarged the photo and pointed to the screen. "It says 'Hemorrhage.'"

LuAnn squinted and saw that it did indeed list hemorrhage as the cause. "So he bled to death?"

"That's what it says," Danny said.

"But why?" LuAnn did some quick calculations. "He was only nineteen years old."

"Unfortunately, this doesn't tell us why," Danny said. "But look. It does tell us his next of kin was his father, Stanley Carroll. Which probably means that he wasn't married, or his wife would have been listed."

"Yes, we know from his birth certificate that his father's name was Stanley," LuAnn said.

"And look. Here you can see where and when he was buried. First Baptist Church, Darbydale. So you can probably assume that's where his family went to church. The church might still have some records. Baptism records or information about the family. The undertaker is listed here as well. If he's still around, his office might have some records about this Jay, if you're interested in that." He rubbed his hands together. "Isn't it wonderful how much this one little piece of paper can tell you?"

LuAnn grinned. "It's a little bit creepy how excited you are about this," she teased.

Danny laughed. "I know, I know. This is a person's life, and it's not to be taken lightly. But I do love learning about the past, and this is such an interesting way to do it."

"I see your point." Under different circumstances, LuAnn probably would have enjoyed spending time digging through the church baptism records and combing through the undertaker's files, looking for any scrap of information about Jay's life and his death. That search for some previously undiscovered piece of the past was in every historian's blood. But right now, LuAnn wasn't focused on all the details of Jay's life.

"How would I find out more about how he died? As in, what caused the hemorrhage?"

"Well, let's see if the obituary tells us anything," Danny said. "Darbydale, Ohio, huh?" He turned to a computer terminal on the desk in front of him and typed in the name of the town. "It looks like we might have the best luck searching the *Grove City Record.*"

"Oh?"

"It was the newspaper published closest to Darbydale. It's out of business now, but it was publishing in the area at the time of Jay's death, so my guess is it's our best bet for an obituary. Let's see."

He typed something into the computer, clicked on a link, and asked, "How do you spell the last name?"

LuAnn spelled the name *Carroll* and saw that he was using a database search engine.

"You have the *Grove City Record* on microfilm?" LuAnn eyed the rows of cabinets along the walls. There were a lot of drawers, but she couldn't imagine there were enough that they could have the archives of every small historical newspaper in the area here.

"No, no," Danny said. "Not here on site. But for some of the smaller papers, we do have access through a database program."

"That's convenient," LuAnn said.

He clicked on a link. "Like I said, we help folks with a lot of genealogy research here. You'd be shocked at how useful these little papers are. Used to be, that was how you shared news, before the internet and TV came in and changed things."

LuAnn wanted to laugh. He had to be young enough to have had internet access when he was in elementary school. But he was an old soul, she supposed, and she liked that.

"Okay. I think I found something," he said and turned his screen so she could see it. "It looks like an obituary."

LuAnn looked at the article he had pulled up on the screen. It was indeed an obituary, with a photo of a clean-cut brown-haired teenager next to it. Jay Aaron Carroll was printed at the top.

Jay Aaron Carroll passed away on August 4, 1968. Just nineteen years old, he is mourned by his parents, Stanley and Arlene Carroll, and his younger brother Miles Carroll. A service for Jay will be held at the First Baptist Church, Darbydale, on August 7. He will be laid to rest at First Baptist Cemetery afterward. Beloved son, brother, and friend, he will be deeply missed.

"Hmm." LuAnn read it through again, looking for clues she'd missed the first time.

"It doesn't give us much we didn't already know, does it?" Danny said, shaking his head.

"Not really."

"Well, let's see if there's anything else." Danny typed something on the screen, and she held her breath. "Ah. Okay, here's another article, from a couple days before." He clicked on the link and grimaced. "Oh. Wow."

Teen Barely Holding on to Life after Threshing Accident, the headline read.

"Yikes." LuAnn read the article. Jay had been harvesting wheat on his family farm and gotten his arm caught in the thresher. His father had turned the machine off, but he was badly mangled, and by the time they made it to the hospital, he had lost a lot of blood. "The poor boy."

"The poor father. Can you imagine?" Danny let out a long breath.

"Well, I guess we know what caused the hemorrhage," she said.

"I guess we do." Danny made a note on the pad next to his computer. "It's not happy news, but it is the answer you were looking for." He turned the screen so she could get a better view. "Does that give you what you need?"

"Not really." Luann thought for a moment, and then she shook her head. "Not exactly."

Danny cocked his head. "So what are you looking for, exactly?"

LuAnn considered how much to say and how to explain what was really going on.

"Okay, here's a curveball. I'm interested in Jay, but not for his own sake. It turns out there's someone we're pretty sure is using his identity, and I'm really interested in finding out how that happened and why."

"Oh. That's easy enough. Well, the first part is anyway. I'm not sure I can help you figure out the why, but the how is probably fairly straightforward." With a glance to ask permission, Danny picked up LuAnn's phone again and moved the photo of the death certificate around. "See this?" He pointed to a small box near the top of the death certificate.

LuAnn squinted. It was a series of numbers. "Looks like a Social Security number."

Danny nodded. "Looks like you got lucky here. They didn't start putting these on all death certificates until a year or two after this. In 1967, it was still dependent on where you were when you died. Looks like Franklin County started using them a bit earlier than most."

"That's great." LuAnn wasn't exactly sure how that helped.

"My guess would be that the guy you're talking about needed a Social Security number for some reason, and he adopted this one, knowing that the original Jay wouldn't be needing it anymore."

"But how would that work?" LuAnn thought for a moment. "He could just start using someone else's Social Security number?"

"And name. And life, basically," Dany confirmed. "You would have to, since the number is attached to the birth certificate."

"Wouldn't the original Jay's family have been mad when they heard someone was using his name?"

"I'm sure they would have if they'd learned about it," he said. "But I'd guess your man moved far away. And this was before the internet, so it's not like they'd just run a Google search and find out about it."

Okay. She supposed it was possible, though she wasn't sure she was totally buying it yet. There was still something that didn't add up.

"But there was a death certificate," LuAnn said. "The state of Ohio knew that the original Jay was dead. How could someone continue to use his Social Security number after that? When you die, doesn't someone notify...I don't know. Whoever keeps track of things like that? So the number can't continue to be used?"

"You'd think so." Danny pursed his lips and thought for a moment. "I'm not sure who does that, though." He took in a breath. "But I think I can find out."

"How?"

"My sister-in-law's father runs a funeral home up in Akron. It's a family business, so she basically grew up at the funeral home."

"Talk about an interesting childhood."

"Yeah, she has some stories. Apparently when you grow up surrounded by corpses you develop something of a dark sense of humor. But she's wonderful."

"You said it's a family business. Does she work there now?"

"No, she managed to escape that fate by marrying my brother. Not sure it's much better, really."

She laughed.

"I think her brother is poised to take over the business someday. But let me give her a call. She might be able to help."

"Please." LuAnn gestured for him to go ahead.

"My phone is downstairs. Let me go call her, and I'll be right back."

As Danny walked out of the room, LuAnn turned back to the article on the screen. She reread the story about Jay's accident. It must have been so awful for his parents, watching their son bleed to death. You would never recover from something like that. She didn't know whether Stanley and Arlene were still alive, but she said a prayer for them anyway.

The screen showed the whole newspaper page where the article had appeared, and she read the headlines. Farmers in the area were gearing up for the county fair. Crowds were gathering outside the Ohio statehouse to protest the ongoing US military presence in Vietnam. A local pastor was trying to get a soup kitchen off the ground. LuAnn was fascinated by the mix of local and international news and by the old-fashioned typefaces and layouts.

"I think I figured out a way this could make sense," Danny said as he came back into the room.

"Oh yeah?" LuAnn felt something like hope.

"I found out that it's usually the undertaker who reports a death to the Social Security Administration."

"That's interesting. I guess I never really thought about who handles things like that."

"The job of an undertaker is starting to sound worse and worse, right? After you deal with the dead body, you get to deal with the government," Danny joked.

LuAnn laughed. "But in this case, it seems the report must not have been made."

"Apparently not. Maybe it wasn't standard for them to do so in those days. Or maybe there's another reason." Danny looked at LuAnn. "Can I see that death certificate again?"

LuAnn opened the image and handed over her phone. Danny noted the name of the funeral parlor and typed it into the search field.

"Ah."

"Ah what?" LuAnn craned her neck to see what he was looking at. Then she saw the article on the screen and understood.

"The funeral home burned down," Danny said.

"With all its records, just a few days after Jay's funeral."

"It's entirely possible the undertaker didn't have a chance to notify the Social Security Administration about Jay's death before all the records were destroyed," Danny said.

"Wow," LuAnn said. "So, I mean, I guess it's plausible that the real Jay died, the federal government was never notified, and the man I know as Jay swooped in and started using the name and Social Security number." She thought for minute. It was possible. Jay was roughly the same age that this original Jay would have been, and if he'd moved to another part of the country, it was unlikely the original Jay's family would have ever found out. "But how would he have found Jay's identity to steal it?"

Danny shrugged. "Hard to say, really, but it could have been any number of ways. Maybe he knew him. Maybe he read the obituary and saw an opportunity."

"But he got really lucky with the fire to be able to pull it off."

"I guess," he said, and LuAnn understood that he was hinting at more. Could he really mean...?

"Or he might have been counting on the fact that different branches of government are not especially good at communicating with each other and hoped that he wouldn't be found out."

"Huh." LuAnn played it all through in her head, and she could see that it was indeed possible. After the man they knew as Jay had taken the original Jay's name and Social Security number, he no doubt adopted all the facts listed on file for Jay.

Jay's birth certificate said he was born in Columbus, Ohio, so the new Jay made that his story—even though, if LuAnn was right, his accent gave him away as being from somewhere else entirely. The man she knew as Jay had made his life match the details of the original Jay's life.

"It doesn't explain why he did it though," Danny said.

"No, it doesn't." LuAnn took in a deep breath. Something niggled at the back of her mind. Something she'd learned in the past few days, something that might be relevant. But she couldn't call it up. She shook her head. "And it doesn't tell us anything about who he was before."

"I'd love to help you figure that out, but I'll need something to go on," Danny said. "Do you have any clues about who he could really be?"

"No," LuAnn said. "I'm afraid I don't." She looked down at the counter, and a moment later, she felt a smile spread across her face. "But I have an idea for how to find out."

LuAnn left the archive building and took a seat on a wooden bench under a beautiful weeping willow on the lawn. It was cool enough in the shade, and there was the slightest hint of a breeze. She pulled her phone out of her purse and dialed her mother's friend Eleanor. Eleanor was bedridden and in the late stages of cancer, so LuAnn wasn't sure if she would be able to have a lengthy conversation, but she thought it was past time to say hello in any case.

"Hello?" Her voice was weak, but it was undeniably Eleanor. She still had that soft, lilting twang.

"Hi, Eleanor. It's LuAnn Sherrill."

"LuAnn. You know, I had the funniest feeling you were going to call me today. And here you are."

LuAnn had long ago given up being surprised by Eleanor's intuition or nudges from the Holy Spirit or whatever it was that made her sometimes know things before they happened. She had always been like that.

"How are you feeling today?"

"Oh, you know. Getting through it."

LuAnn knew she must be in pain and admired Eleanor's bravery.

"Daytime television is awful though," Eleanor said. "That's the worst part of all this. For so many years I would have given anything to stay home and lie in bed all day, and now that I can do it, there's nothing good to watch."

LuAnn laughed. Eleanor still had her sense of humor, at least.

"But you didn't call to hear me go on about nonsense. What's going on?"

"I actually had a strange question," LuAnn said.

"Lay it on me."

"There's a man staying here at the inn, and I'm sure I know him from somewhere. I think we've met before, and I'm pretty sure it was when I was young, because he accidentally called me Lulu."

"Oh wow."

"He says we haven't met, but I don't believe him. And I was wondering if you knew of anyone it could be. Anyone who came into the diner regularly, maybe, or anyone who was a friend of my mother's."

"What is his name?"

"Well, he goes by Jay Carroll now, but I don't think that was his name at the time."

"Hmm. What does he look like?"

LuAnn described him, but even as she did, she realized how pointless it was. Jay looked like a man in his seventies now, but surely he hadn't looked that way fifty years ago.

"I'm afraid that's not much to go on," Eleanor said.

"No, I suppose it's not."

"I can't think of anyone who would fit that description, but I will think about it," Eleanor promised.

"Thank you," LuAnn said. They chatted for a while longer, and then LuAnn hung up. It had been worth a try, she supposed, but it didn't feel like she was any closer to finding out who Jay really was.

CHAPTER FOURTEEN

When LuAnn got back to the inn, she found Janice in the basement, giving the space a once-over before the tour that afternoon. The ceilings down there were low, and the space was dimly lit with yellowish light from a few old-fashioned fixtures hanging from the ceiling. They'd updated the wiring when they renovated the inn, but they hadn't spent much on modernizing the basement aside from installing a commercial laundry room, and the space always felt moldy and damp to LuAnn.

"Hi there," Janice said. She had a feather duster in one hand and a garbage bag in the other. LuAnn wanted to laugh at the idea of going over this dank, dark basement—a laundry room, old servants' quarters, and a claustrophobic tunnel to the river—with a pink feather duster, but she held her tongue. It couldn't hurt to make sure the place looked as nice as possible for their guests, who did seem to be used to the highest levels of service. "How did it go at the archive room?"

"It was . . . Well, it was interesting," LuAnn said. She explained what she'd learned about how the man they knew as Jay had probably seized upon the dead man's Social Security number.

Janice nodded. "That makes sense. I was thinking it must be something like that."

"You were?" LuAnn cocked her head.

"Well, I guessed it might have to do with needing a Social Security number," Janice said. "Isn't that what these things are always about?"

LuAnn didn't know what kind of things of this nature Janice was used to, but this was all new to LuAnn. But before she could ask, Janice said, "So, I had an interesting conversation with Jacqueline this morning."

"You did?" Jacqueline must think they were the chattiest innkeepers in history.

"The group was gathering in the lobby, and Jacqueline and Jay came down," Janice said. After giving the area a final appraising glance, she gestured for LuAnn to follow her into the laundry room. This room was bright and clean, with three industrial-sized washing machines and three dryers, shelves with gallons of detergent and bleach and stain remover, and a large table in the middle for folding and sorting. "I went over and said I'd heard Jay wasn't feeling well and asked if he was doing any better," Janice said.

"Did he look sick?" The load of towels in one of the dryers was done, so LuAnn emptied it onto the table and started folding.

"Not especially," Janice said. "I mean, it's hard to say. He doesn't look like a spring chicken. But he didn't seem noticeably ill."

"Hmm." LuAnn set a folded towel in the laundry basket.

"It could have been something not visible that was bothering him," Janice said as she bent over to open the washing machine door.

"Or it was possible he simply wanted to avoid me this morning," LuAnn said. She folded another towel. She was glad they'd sprung for the good-quality towels. They were thick and fluffy and held up to repeated washings. "Hard to say."

"In any case, I asked where they were off to this morning." Janice pulled out a load of the wet laundry and set it into the open dryer. "I knew they were going to Mound Cemetery, but I wanted to see what they said."

"And what did they say?"

"Well, Jay didn't say much, but then I was expecting that." Janice fished out the rest of the wet sheets and loaded them into the dryer. "But Jacqueline started going on about how much she loved cemeteries."

"That's kind of odd."

Janice smiled. "Oh, I don't know. I enjoy a nice walk through a peaceful cemetery myself. As long as it's not nighttime. In that case, keep me away." She shivered.

LuAnn stopped folding and turned to her.

"Don't tell me you're afraid of ghosts."

"No." Janice stepped toward the table. "Of course not. Ghosts aren't real, I know that. When we die, we don't hang around here. But, I don't know, there's something kind of scary about being surrounded by dead people at night, isn't there?"

"Not unless you're afraid they're going to get you somehow." LuAnn wanted to laugh. "I mean, otherwise, they're just lying there in their graves. Do you think they creep out at night and sneak up on people or something?"

"Of course not." Janice set her jaw. "Now you're just being silly. I didn't say anything of the sort. All I'm saying is that I don't like being in cemeteries after dark. In *any* case, the point is that Jacqueline was excited about the cemetery because she's really into genealogy, and apparently graveyards are great sources for finding information about ancestors and such."

"Does she have ancestors in the area?" LuAnn went back to folding the towel in her hands.

"I don't think so. I think she just likes cemeteries because they've been useful to her in the past." Janice reached for a towel and shook it out. "Then she started talking about how she'd traced her family history back a couple hundred years, when her great-great-great-grandfather started a tobacco plantation or something."

"Yikes." LuAnn's thoughts went back to the tunnel that led to the river just a few feet from here. Jacqueline was very proud of her family's history, that was clear, but LuAnn wondered if the wealth she was enjoying now was built on the backs of slaves. Had any of the workers at that tobacco plantation passed through these tunnels on the way to freedom?

"Yeah. I didn't want to get into the subject of generational wealth and all that, so I asked about whether she'd also traced Jay's family." She folded the towel she was holding in half. "And here's where it gets interesting."

"What did she say?" LuAnn set the folded towel into the basket and reached for the next one.

"She said that Jay wasn't into genealogy. Well, actually, no, it was a lot stronger than that. What she said was that Jay had refused to cooperate, even though she was trying to build a family tree for their kids. Which I thought was interesting, given what you told us earlier."

"It makes sense, I guess. If he won't even talk about his family, why would he want her building his family tree?"

"She told me she tried to coerce him into doing one of those swab kits where they use your saliva to tell you where your ancestors are from, and he flat out refused." Janice smiled. "Jay was listening to us and said that those things are government conspiracies, and they just want your DNA so they can own a piece of you."

"Really?" LuAnn laughed. "I've thought of doing one of those tests. It would be interesting to see where my ancestors came from."

"Yeah, well, I think Jay might have been overreacting a teensy bit, but there are privacy issues with those tests. Part of it is because the other thing those tests do for you is allow you to compare your DNA to others in their database, and they match you with people who you're likely related to based on your results."

"Oh, that's right. I've heard stories of people finding out they're adopted or that their father wasn't really their father because of those tests."

"They're great for reuniting adoptees with birth mothers and finding long-lost relatives. But terrible if you want to keep it quiet that you're living someone else's life. It would only take a little bit of research to find that Jay Carroll wasn't related to anyone else with that last name," Janice said.

"So his reticence makes a ton of sense," LuAnn said.

"Absolutely. And given what you found at the archives today, I think it's very safe to assume that he desperately does not want his wife and family to know that he was not born Jay Carroll and that he stole the name and identification from a young man who died."

"Underscoring the idea that Jacqueline has no idea about any of this," LuAnn said.

"Right." Janice finished folding the towel into a neat square. How did she always manage to get it so perfect? "Which brings us back to the question of why he changed his name in the first place."

"Right." LuAnn reached for the next towel. "And I haven't gotten anywhere on that."

"I haven't either, but I did a quick Google search on prison breaks from the late 1960s."

"You think he broke out of prison?"

"I don't have any idea. Just trying to check out any and all possibilities." She picked up a towel and made a neat crease down the middle, folding it in half perfectly. "As you've pointed out, he must have had a reason to need a new name and a new life. Covering up a criminal past—and being wanted on a felony—would be a pretty decent reason to start your life over."

"True enough. Well, did you find any?"

"There was one in West Virginia in 1969 where two men convicted of robbing a bank broke out."

LuAnn shook her head. "The timing doesn't work. He was already in the army using the name Jay Carroll by that point."

"Right. Well, it turns out it's not all that common that someone escapes from prison."

"I suppose that's a good thing."

"I'd say so. In any case, the only other prison break I could find that might be relevant was in 1966, but the man was caught and sentenced to life in prison."

"So it seems it's not likely that's why he changed his name," LuAnn said.

"That doesn't mean that he isn't a criminal," Janice said. "Just that without knowing who he really is, I don't know how to look up whether he has a criminal record or not."

Once again, something pricked at the back of LuAnn's mind. There was something there, if only she could unearth it...She thought for a minute, trying to think through everything she knew about Jay.

"The first record we have of him is from January 1969," LuAnn said.

Janice nodded. "I think that's right. That's when he joined the army."

LuAnn thought back through what Tess had said when she'd told them about what she'd learned. "He enlisted."

Janice nodded, her lips pursed. LuAnn wasn't sure what she was trying to get at either, but she would work it out by talking aloud. She continued.

"Not too many people were enlisting in the army in January 1969," she said. LuAnn had only been a teenager, but she vividly remembered the news headlines and video footage of planes flying low over the jungle and protesters marching on

Washington. LuAnn hadn't been about to grow her hair long and run off to the streets of San Francisco, but she had friends who were very involved in the protests, and she remembered the indignation and fear that gripped so many Americans during that time.

"It was before the draft," Janice said. "The first draft lottery took place on December 1, 1969."

"So he joined up voluntarily, in theory at least. But again, it wasn't like this was World War II when men were clamoring to do their part. He joined the army, surely knowing that he would be sent off to fight in a war that a large percentage of the public thought was unjust." LuAnn mulled this over.

"I'm sure people had all kinds of reasons for joining the army then," Janice said. "It's a noble calling, and some people dream of being a soldier their whole lives."

"You're right, of course," LuAnn said. "But there are also plenty of people who join up because they need to, for some reason. They don't have any job prospects at home. Or they need a new start."

"You're suggesting that Jay joined the army as a way to get a new start with his new name?"

"I'm tossing it out there as a theory. That for whatever reason, he took this new identity, and then he joined the army. It would mean getting far away from whatever it was he'd left behind, and far away from the real Jay's family. It would mean a purpose and a way to build a new life."

"It would mean years sweltering in a jungle fighting for an uncertain cause."

LuAnn shrugged. "Maybe it seemed like a fair price to pay. And"—she felt a thrill of excitement pass through her—"I bet you need a Social Security number to join the military. Which could explain why he needed to take a new identity, to get a new number."

Janice kept folding as she thought, but then she said, "But the army is a government organization. Wouldn't they have made sure the guy who enlisted wasn't, you know, using the Social Security number of a dead guy?"

"But the real Jay's death wasn't reported to the federal government, remember?" LuAnn felt more and more sure she was right. "And maybe the army was so eager for volunteers willing to be soldiers at that time that they didn't always double-check all the paperwork as thoroughly as they should have."

"That's some serious speculation." Janice eyed her doubtfully.

"You're right, I don't have a way to prove any of it. But it feels right. And in any case, it's true that the first actual record we know of for the new Jay is when he joined the army in January 1969."

"And the real Jay died in August 1968," Janice said. "So sometime in that window, the man we know as Jay adopted his identity." She was quiet for a minute, and then she let out a sigh. "But we still don't know why he changed his name or who he was before."

"No," LuAnn agreed. "But we're getting closer."

"We are?"

"I have an idea."

"Hold on to your hat."

"He called me Lulu."

Janice cocked her head. "Really?" Janice understood the significance of that, LuAnn knew. She'd known LuAnn in kindergarten, when many people had called her Lulu. "How did he know?"

"He tried to play it off like it was a joke, like of course people call me Lulu, but I don't know. We certainly don't know each other well enough to give each other nicknames, you know? I think it slipped out without his meaning it to."

"Because he knew you back when you were Lulu."

"I think so."

"Wow." Janice set the towel down.

"And then he avoided me at breakfast."

"He didn't come down, did he?"

"No. I think he was hiding so he didn't have to face me."

"Okay. So he obviously doesn't want you to know how he knows you. So how are you going to find that out?"

"I found my mother's old photo albums in the storage unit, and I'm going to look through—"

Just then, they heard footsteps on the stairs, and they looked up to see Tess hurrying down the steps, her laptop clutched in her arms.

"What's the matter?" LuAnn asked. It wasn't like Tess to come thundering down the stairs like this, and the look on her face made it clear something important had happened.

"You guys," Tess said. Her cheeks were red, and her auburn hair was coming loose from her short ponytail on one side. "You'll never guess what I found."

CHAPTER FIFTEEN

January 15, 1860

Prudence could not believe it when Jason slipped the letter into her hand.

"This was waiting for thee in town," he said.

Prudence did not recognize the cramped, slanted writing. But she knew. The thick grayish paper, nothing like the delicate creamy stationery Jason's mother used, took her back to her childhood. And the postmark from Hancock County.

"I thank thee," Prudence said. She wanted to tear the envelope open right there, immediately, but she waited. She wanted to be alone to read whatever news the letter might contain.

She tried to calm the fluttering in her breast and listen as Jason talked about an interaction he'd had in town. But when he went into the bedroom to change his clothes, she stood and headed toward the door.

"Moses, come." The child had recently learned to crawl, and now he was scooting himself all over the place. She had to keep a close eye on him. He pushed himself across the floor now, and she scooped him up and set him down in a patch of grass under the apple tree in the yard. It was the first warm day of spring, the kind of day that promised the early buds would arrive soon.

Prudence slid her finger under the seal of the envelope and carefully lifted out the paper inside. She sucked in a breath as she read.

Surely…

No, it couldn't be.

CHAPTER SIXTEEN

LuAnn and Janice huddled around the computer that Tess had set on the coffee table in the lobby of the inn. After she'd found them in the basement, they'd all come up to the first floor and gathered around the laptop.

"Okay," Tess said, opening the lid. "I was supposed to be getting the rooms ready for Lauren and her fiancé and her dad, but I kept thinking about the mystery surrounding Jay and about your missing wallet, and I kept feeling like there was something I was missing. Some connection between the two that I should have seen. So I decided to go back and watch that security camera footage again."

"Wait. You're not telling me you found out that Jay was behind the wallet thefts after all?" LuAnn couldn't see how that was possible. The man in the museum security camera footage clearly wasn't Jay.

"No." Tess shook her head as the grainy black-and-white security footage filled the screen again. "It's not him. There's no way it could be. But there was something about this guy"— she froze the image on the computer screen just as the wallet thief came into the shot—"that kept nagging at me. That kept making me think of Jay somehow."

LuAnn looked at the figure again. His face was covered by the hat, and it was hard to tell much of anything about him aside from the fact that he was younger and thinner than Jay.

"What is it?" Janice sounded as bewildered as LuAnn felt.

Tess pointed at the man's shirt. "See this?"

"That black dot?" LuAnn had noticed the small black spot on the chest of the white polo shirt, but she hadn't thought anything of it. Most clothing these days had some kind of brand or logo on it, didn't it?

"I figured it was an alligator or a penguin or whatever they're putting on name-brand clothes these days," Janice said.

"That's what I thought at first too," Tess said. "But something about it seemed familiar, so I zoomed in to check it out anyway." She used the arrow tool on the screen to zoom in on that area of the image. All LuAnn could make out was a grayish blob.

"Does that mean anything to you?" Janice asked, looking at LuAnn, who shook her head.

"It gets blurrier as you make it bigger," Tess said, zooming out again. Now it was clearer but smaller, and LuAnn still had no idea what it was supposed to represent. "But I used this photo editing program I have to sharpen it."

"You have photo editing software?" LuAnn cocked her head.

"Not anything professional. Just enough to clean up pictures of my grandkids," Tess said with a smile. LuAnn should have guessed. Tess's daughter Lizzie had four-year-old triplets, and Tess loved spending time with them. "But check this out."

She clicked on another window, and a clearer version of the photo emerged. She had done that with just this photo editing software? LuAnn still didn't recognize the logo, but it was much clearer.

She squinted at the screen. "Is that the same picture?" It seemed to show a crest of some kind.

"It is," Tess said. "And guess what it's a picture of?"

"I have no idea," Janice said.

"It took me a while, but then I realized why I was thinking of Jay. When we googled him that first day, what did we learn about him?"

"That he has a nice house," Janice said.

"No." Tess shook her head. "Look. It's Pinecrest Golf Club," she said, referring to a golf course just over the river in West Virginia. "That's their logo."

"Is it?" LuAnn had to admit she'd never paid much attention to the golf clubs in the area. She'd played a game or two of golf in the past but found it mind-numbingly dull.

"It is." Tess opened another window and pulled up the website for the Pinecrest Golf Club. There it was, right there in the top right corner of the website. A logo just like the one in the photo. LuAnn didn't need to ask how Tess had recognized it. Tess didn't play golf, but her late husband, Jeffrey, had managed a golf club in Stow. She'd no doubt spent so much of her life around the club that she'd gotten to know the other clubs in the area.

"But we found out that Jay is a member of a country club in Lexington," Janice said, shaking her head.

"That's right," Tess said. "And that's what made me think of this. I'd seen the logo of his club, and it was a lot like this one, except instead of just having two golf clubs crossed at the top, his club had an eagle over the two clubs. But when I saw it on the screen the other day when we were researching Jay, it reminded me of the logo for the Pinecrest Club."

LuAnn saw the logic of it, sort of. But she was still impressed. She never would have gotten there herself. "And if he's wearing a shirt with the logo, that likely means he's a member of the club."

"Or he works there," Janice suggested.

"That's possible," Tess said. "Maybe he came before or after his shift. But in any case, he's connected to the club in some way."

"Which means we should be able to figure out how," LuAnn said, slowly understanding what Tess was getting at.

"Exactly." Tess was trying to hold back a smile. "How long do we have until we're supposed to give the tour of the basement?"

LuAnn glanced at the antique mantel clock next to the painting of the inn from a hundred years ago. "An hour and a half."

"Plenty of time," Tess said, meeting LuAnn's eye.

"Would you be okay if Tess and I popped over to the club for a bit?" LuAnn asked Janice.

"Just make sure you're back in time for the tour," Janice said. "There's no way I'm going to show them that creepy tunnel on my own."

LuAnn laughed. "We'll be back." She looked at Tess. "Are you ready to go?"

"As soon as I grab my purse."

A few minutes later, they had crossed the river and parked in front of the Pinecrest Golf and Country Club. The clubhouse was in a building of stacked stone with tasteful white shutters and a large wooden door. The flower beds in the parking area were blooming with petunias and sundrops, and the grass around the building was perfectly manicured. Large azalea bushes bloomed in brilliant pink along the fence at the far side of the parking lot.

"Nice place," LuAnn said.

"It's about what I'd expect," Tess said and led the way across the pavement toward the front door. LuAnn thought it was funny how comfortable Tess seemed in this setting. She was so down-to-earth and laid-back, and it wasn't like she frequented places like this. But LuAnn supposed that after spending most of her life around a golf club, she'd lost the sense of intimidation that kept LuAnn hanging back even now.

"Welcome to Pinecrest. How can I help you?" A young man in a white polo shirt with the now-familiar logo stood behind a wide wooden desk. He was probably in college, if LuAnn had to guess, and had floppy brown hair streaked with blond.

"Hello," Tess said. "This place is so lovely."

LuAnn looked around, taking in the vaulted wood ceilings and the large windows along the back wall that looked out over a deep green fairway. Behind the desk, she saw an open door, and behind it the edge of a massive desk. It must be an office.

"My husband used to manage a club, in Stow. It was nice, but it wasn't as beautiful as this."

"That's awesome," the young man said. "I think I've heard of that one. It's supposed to be a nice club. I've never been there myself, but I've heard it's got one of the toughest sand traps around."

"It is notoriously tricky," Tess said. She glanced around. "Oh, my. Jeffrey would have loved this place." She sighed and then added, "He passed away a few years ago, and he always wanted to visit more clubs out this way."

LuAnn watched in awe as Tess established a connection to the club before appealing to the young man's sympathies.

"I'm sorry for your loss," the young man said. He didn't seem to know what else to say, but after a brief pause, Tess jumped in.

"Well, I'm glad to be here, but I'm afraid it's in something of a strange circumstance. I actually wondered if you might be able to help me. I'm trying to figure out who this man is, and I believe he has some connection to the club."

Tess pulled out her phone and showed him a still of the museum's security camera footage. She'd zoomed in a bit, and it wasn't obvious at first glance where the picture had come from.

"Oh, yeah, that's Gary." He squinted at the photo. "From maintenance."

LuAnn couldn't believe it. Could it really have been this simple after all?

"He works here then?" Tess asked.

"Yeah. Do you want me to call him?"

"Oh, no, that's quite all right," Tess said at the same moment a man in a button-down and tie came out of the office.

"Is there something I can help you with?" he said, looking from LuAnn to Tess and back again. LuAnn sensed he'd overhead the whole conversation, and the look on his face said he wasn't thrilled about what had just happened.

"Oh no, thank you," Tess said quickly. "We're good. Thank you."

And before LuAnn knew what was happening, Tess had turned and was hurrying toward the door.

"Thank you," LuAnn called over her shoulder, hurrying after her.

"That was an abrupt departure," she said when she caught up with Tess, who was already buckling herself into the driver's seat of her car.

"That poor kid. He's about to get chewed out, I'm afraid," Tess said. She turned on the engine, and cool air started to pour out of the vents. "In places like this, discretion is of supreme importance. He should not have told us what he just did."

"It's not like he told us all about a member," LuAnn said.

"Doesn't matter." Tess checked the rearview mirror before she backed up. "But it will be a learning experience for him, I guess. And, on the plus side, we know who our thief is."

"I can't believe it," LuAnn said. "After all the hassle and investigating, all it took was recognizing one little logo." She looked over at Tess. "Thank you."

"Thank Jeffrey," Tess said. "It drove me nuts how obsessed he was with measuring up to the other golf clubs in the area, but I guess in the end it paid off."

LuAnn glanced at the clock on the dashboard. They still had almost forty minutes before the tour was supposed to start. "Should we swing by the police station before we head back to the inn?"

"I think that's a very good idea." Tess waited for a white pickup to pass before she pulled onto the road. "I think Gary from maintenance is about to get a rude awakening."

LuAnn smiled. They'd caught him. Or, they would catch him, as soon as they told the police what they knew.

"There's one mystery solved," Tess said.

LuAnn laughed. "Yes, I suppose so. But it doesn't get us any closer to figuring out who in the world Jay is or how I know him."

"No, it doesn't," Tess said. "But we're getting closer. I feel like there's going to be a breakthrough any moment now."

"I sure hope so," LuAnn said. "We don't have a lot of moments left. The tour group checks out tomorrow." She didn't know what she'd do if they didn't figure the answer out before then. She had always been invested in solving the mysteries that had come up since they'd moved into the inn. Her mind loved puzzles, and she often found that she couldn't stop herself from thinking about the mysteries until they'd figured out the answers. But this one was different. This one was personal. This man—this whole thing—was tied in with her past somehow, and if she didn't find answers, she didn't know if she'd ever be able to rest.

"We'll get it figured out before then," Tess promised. "Just wait. You'll see."

LuAnn nodded. She just hoped Tess was right.

CHAPTER SEVENTEEN

By the time they'd explained to three different people at the police station how they figured out that the wallet thief was named Gary and that he worked in maintenance at the Pinecrest Club, it was past time for the tour to start, and they rushed home and found Janice, surrounded by Meaghan and Alex and all eight guests, gathered at the bottom of the stairs in the basement. Janice was in the middle of explaining how they'd discovered Prudence Willard's diary when they'd started renovating the inn and how they'd uncovered the secret history of the inn. She smiled as Tess and LuAnn hurried down the stairs, but her eyes were steely.

"I'm so sorry we missed the beginning of the tour," LuAnn said, hoping the cheerfulness in her voice would compensate for the frustration in Janice's gaze. "But it sounds like Janice was doing a great job of explaining the history of the inn."

"I was just about to explain how they came to use these rooms down here for hiding runaway slaves," Janice said. She gave Tess a significant look.

"How about I tell them that?" Tess had gotten the hint, and she immediately started to talk about how Prudence Willard, along with a handful of other workers at the inn, had kept the slaves in the tiny basement rooms that were also used for regular staff, including free blacks, and how it was often impossible for the authorities to tell the difference.

"So they hid them in plain sight?" Mona from Arizona asked.

"Sometimes," LuAnn jumped in. "More often, they kept them down here for as short a time as possible. They fed them and treated any injuries and then sent them on their way as quickly as possible, usually under the cover of night."

"We know from Prudence's diary that she became friendly with some of them," Tess said. "But we also know that it was incredibly dangerous, and that she and her family and the others who worked here had to use their wits more than once to throw the authorities off the trail."

"Why don't you go ahead and take a look at the rooms," Janice said, gesturing for them to head down the hallway. At the far end, the door to the garden let in small squares of light, but the hallway was still small and dimly lit.

While the guests moved on down to look at the half-dozen small spare rooms, LuAnn and Tess walked over to Janice.

"We're so sorry," Tess said.

"We didn't mean to make you start without us," LuAnn said. "But wait until you hear what happened."

Janice listened as Tess and LuAnn told her about finding the identity of the wallet thief, and Janice's frustration melted away as she realized that they'd solved that mystery.

"I can't believe you really figured it out," Janice said. "Before the police."

"Before the police." Tess smiled, trying to get Janice to smile in return. Janice wouldn't go that far, but she was meeting their eyes again.

"Well, at least you made it back before I had to show them the tunnel itself," Janice said with a sniff.

LuAnn laughed. Janice's claustrophobia kicked in just looking at the narrow earthen tunnel to the river.

They let the guests explore the rooms for a moment longer, and then LuAnn gathered them in the room that held the secret entrance to the tunnel itself. She explained that they always kept the door locked on the other end, and guests were usually not allowed anywhere near it, but that they were letting them take a look because they were part of the special Thatch tour.

The tunnel entrance was hidden behind a small stool cleverly attached to a panel in the wall. Tess pulled the stool away from the wall, and the opening to the tunnel appeared. Of course, they wouldn't permit the guests to actually enter the tunnel. LuAnn got a lump in her throat, just like she did every time she saw it. It was incredible to think that this little tunnel had been instrumental in allowing so many enslaved people to escape to freedom. So often, when they talked about the history of this inn and the Underground Railroad in general, they focused on the bravery of people like Prudence, who risked their families and their livelihoods to aid the travelers. But looking at the tunnel now, LuAnn couldn't help but think about the slaves themselves, about the horrors they must have faced that led them to risk their lives to escape captivity, and the bravery it must have taken to make it this far. Or the sheer daring it would have taken to plunge into this narrow tunnel, praying to find a friendly face on the other end.

LuAnn watched as Jay and Jacqueline stepped forward to peer into the tunnel, but while Jacqueline carried on about how dark it was and how long it might be all the way to the river, Jay said nothing. LuAnn kept an eye on him, and after everyone had had a chance to take a look, Tess replaced the panel, and they headed back upstairs. LuAnn waited while everyone else trudged up the stairs, and then she looked around one last time before she headed up.

When she got upstairs, the tour group was starting to make their way up the staircase to get ready for dinner. Tess was chatting with Meaghan. Janice gestured for LuAnn to come over.

"I'm sorry again for not making it—"

Janice waved her words off. "You're forgiven, but that's not what I wanted to say. I heard something."

"Heard what?"

"When we were downstairs, that guy who always wears plaid—"

"Roger," LuAnn said.

"Right. He was talking to Jay—"

"Roger doesn't seem all that chatty."

"He's not, unless you get him on the right topic. But listen. He was talking to Jay about the angle of the tunnel. Jay seemed to only be half listening, but if he'd paid more attention he would have gotten an interesting physics lesson. Anyway, Jay said something, and I almost didn't catch it, but I'm pretty sure I heard right."

"What did he say?"

"He called the tunnel a 'drift.'"

"A drift?" Something caught at the back of her mind, but she couldn't pull it out. "What does that mean?"

"There was a guy in our church, years ago, who was a miner before he retired to live in Marietta. His wife had passed away, and in his later days, I spent a lot of time just talking with him."

LuAnn often forgot how much of Janice's life had been wrapped up in ministering to the people of her husband's congregation.

"He especially liked to talk about his younger days, as most of us do, and he talked a lot about his time working in the mines out in Western Pennsylvania. And I distinctly remember him referring to a tunnel in a mine as a drift."

LuAnn thought about what Janice was saying. "And Jay referred to our tunnel as a drift."

"I don't think he meant to. He made a face when it came out that made me think he hadn't intended to say it. Roger didn't notice, of course, but I heard it, and I wondered."

"That's interesting." It made sense, of course. If he'd known LuAnn when she was a girl, there was a good chance he'd been involved in mining, as so many of LuAnn's mother's extended family and friends were. That was pretty much the main source of employment for so many in the small towns in the Appalachians. Really, it just confirmed what she'd already basically known—that he was somehow connected to the people and places of her early life. But it still didn't get her any closer to figuring out how.

"Does that help at all?" Janice asked.

LuAnn let out a sigh. "Yes and no." LuAnn wished, more than anything, that she could ask her mother about Jay. Her mom would be able to tell her how she'd known Jay. She'd recognize him, or she would know the right questions to ask to figure out how she knew him.

"It's going to drive you nuts, isn't it?"

"It's more than that." LuAnn couldn't articulate how or why, but she had a feeling that this was important somehow.

But if he'd had something to do with mining, that at least gave her a place to start. She was more convinced than ever that Jay was somehow connected to her early life, probably from her childhood in West Virginia. She thought of all those photo albums her mom had kept. Maybe there would be some answers in one of those.

LuAnn was about to start up the stairs, but just then the front door opened, and a young woman walked in, followed by an older man, and, a step behind them, a young man with close-cropped hair. LuAnn recognized the woman immediately. She looked just like the photos Brad had shown of her. She was strikingly pretty, with long dark hair pulled back in a ponytail and a splash of freckles over her nose. She was tall and thin, sporty, and she walked with an effortless kind of grace.

LuAnn smiled and walked toward her. "You must be Lauren."

"Hello." She waved. "You must be LuAnn. Brad said you were pretty, and he was right."

LuAnn felt a flush creep up her cheeks. Had Brad really said that? "Come in, come in," she said quickly, trying to cover her excitement. She gestured for the others to step farther into the lobby. "Welcome to Wayfarers Inn."

"Hi. I'm Mark Haywood." Lauren's father stepped forward. His brown beard and mustache were threaded with gray, and he was tall and thin, almost wiry.

"And I'm Ethan Hansen." Ethan set down the bags he'd been carrying and stepped forward to hold out his hand. He was handsome, no doubt about it. But there was also a kind of gentleness in his voice that she hadn't expected. "Thank you so much for all you're doing for us. We can't tell you how much we appreciate it."

"We're glad to do it. Brad is so happy for you guys." It was almost true, LuAnn thought.

LuAnn wasn't sure what she'd been expecting, really. Based on what Brad had said, she guessed she'd been expecting someone coarse and rude. But Ethan seemed to be gentle and polite, at least on first impression.

"I know it was a lot to pull together quickly," he said.

"It's true that there is usually more time to plan a wedding," LuAnn said. "But it's been no trouble at all."

Lauren put her arm around Ethan's waist. "I know it seems fast, but I just don't see the point of waiting, you know? Once you know it's right."

"Plus, I'll feel better knowing you're officially on my insurance while I'm gone." Ethan put his arm around Lauren's shoulders. "And this way, you can live on base and have the support of other army wives."

Again, LuAnn was taken aback. Based on what Brad had said, she'd expected Ethan to be more flighty, more self-absorbed. But here he was, worried about things like insurance. LuAnn couldn't think of too many young men who considered things of that sort.

"This place is amazing." Lauren was walking around the lobby, taking in the stone mantel over the fireplace, the wall of bookshelves, the baby grand piano, and the big windows. "Is this really where the reception is going to be? It's like a dream. Uncle Brad really came through, didn't he?"

"He always does," Mark said, smiling at Lauren.

"We were actually thinking that with the number of guests you're expecting, it would make sense to have the tables set up under the trees outside. Would you like to go see?"

"Yes, please." Lauren followed LuAnn through the lobby and out the back door, and Mark and Ethan followed behind. They crossed the flagstone patio.

"We were thinking we'd set the buffet tables up on this patio here," LuAnn said. "And then we'll put the dining tables out under those trees." She gestured toward the shady lawn under the live oaks.

"That will be just beautiful," Lauren said.

"Would you like to take a look at the menu or the flowers we've picked out?" LuAnn asked.

She fully expected Lauren to say yes, despite Brad's insistence that she didn't care, but she was surprised when Lauren said, "Maybe later. We're supposed to go meet the pastor who's doing the ceremony in a little while, and I promised Ethan I'd show him around town and take him to my favorite ice cream shop."

"All right then." Lauren really was quite an unusual bride, LuAnn thought, to choose ice cream over seeing the details of her wedding reception. Could Brad be right? Was it possible she really didn't care? "Why don't I get you checked in so you can get settled before you have to go out."

A few minutes later, she'd given Mark a key to Woodsmoke and Pine and gotten Ethan checked in to Maple and Mum. Lauren would be staying in the honeymoon suite, where Ethan would join her after the wedding.

After they went upstairs, LuAnn puzzled over the group. Lauren was just like Brad had said—cheerful, laid-back, and easy-to-please. But could he really be right about Lauren but so far off about Ethan?

She would have to wait and see how it all panned out. Right now, she heard the delivery truck pulling into the loading dock. That would be Marcus, Winnie's grandson, delivering the food for the wedding. She'd better go clear out some space in the fridge.

A half hour later, after LuAnn had put away the food, she went to her car and unloaded the photo albums and bins of home movies. She set the tub of movie rolls in her bedroom, then settled down on the couch in the sitting room on the fourth floor with a stack of photo albums in front of her. Tess had gone over to Lizzie's home to babysit while Lizzie and her husband went to some end-of-the-school-year event, and Janice was at the stove, chopping basil. The sweet, earthy aroma filled the space.

"Are those your mother's?" Janice asked.

"Yes." LuAnn wasn't sure where to even begin. "The ones I got from the storage unit this morning."

"Maybe there are answers inside."

"Let's hope so," LuAnn said. She picked up the book on top and opened the front cover. It was covered in cheap blue vinyl and filled with plastic sleeves that had warped and yellowed over the years. The photos inside were from the eighties, LuAnn guessed, based on the hairstyles and the clothing. She had been engaged to Jesse at this point. That probably explained why the pictures were mostly of the diner and the people who frequented it. Mother had finally moved out of the old apartment that had been their home for so many years, and there were a number of photos of the new house, a small but charming four square home just a few blocks from the main intersection in town. She turned the page and saw a picture of herself and Jesse, arm in arm by the lake, LuAnn laughing. She pressed her lips together. She remembered that day. This was shortly after they'd gotten engaged, and they'd brought Mother and Eleanor out to the lake to spend the day with them. They'd laughed a lot and talked about the future, and…LuAnn shook her head. They'd had no idea.

She turned the page and saw more photos of their courtship, and then—she sucked in a breath. There was a shot of LuAnn modeling the wedding dress Mother had sewn for her.

It had huge puffy sleeves and a sweetheart neckline of shiny white satin, and it was dripping with lace. It would be considered gaudy now, but at the time it was the most beautiful dress she'd ever seen, and her mother had stitched every seam herself. LuAnn shook her head. She couldn't help but wonder, once again, how her life might have been different if Jesse hadn't died...But she knew, from long years of wondering, that it would do her no good to go down that rabbit trail right now. She turned the page and saw pictures of a vacation to Florida and more shots of her mother's new home, and then she set that photo album aside. It was fun to look at the old photos, but she needed something older, from back when she'd been called Lulu.

She reached for an album covered in white faux-leather that was flaking off. This was more like it. On the first page there was a formal wedding portrait of her mom and dad. Her mother wore a sweeping floor-length gown with full sleeves and a high neck, and a long white veil was held in place by flowers. Father wore a dark suit and tie, his hair slicked back. They looked so young and hopeful.

LuAnn turned the page and found a photo of the wedding party. Her mother had had her sister Barbara and a woman LuAnn didn't recognize—a friend, no doubt long forgotten—standing with her, holding bouquets of daisies and baby's breath. Luann recognized her father's brothers standing next to him.

On the next page, Dad stood alone with his family, flanked by a brother on each side, and LuAnn's grandparents beside them. Mother had done a good job of keeping LuAnn connected with her grandparents on her father's side even after Dad left, but after they'd passed away, LuAnn had mostly lost touch with his side of the family.

On the next page, there was a shot of Mom in the middle of her family. LuAnn's aunt Barbara stood on one side of her, and her mother's three brothers stood on the other side, with her grandparents on the end. She studied each face in turn. Aunt Barbara had stayed in the little town outside of Charleston when she'd grown up and had four children with a man who left her for a cocktail waitress. She'd passed away many years ago. And all of LuAnn's uncles were gone too—the eldest, Elmer, to heart failure in his fifties; the youngest, Jack, just a boy in this picture, in an accident in his early twenties; and Donald in assisted living just a few years ago. Seeing their faces now brought back so many memories of family gatherings and holidays in the years after LuAnn and her mother had moved back to West Virginia.

She turned the page, and there was a black-and-white photo of herself as a baby, tacked to the page with photo corners. She was wearing a beautiful frilly dress, and her hair—blond, back then—curled gently around her face. Following that was a family portrait, taken a few years later in some kind of studio. Mother looked radiant in a knee-length dress, her hair curled around her face, and her father wore a suit and tie. LuAnn had to have been about four. She wore a pleated dress with a Peter Pan collar, and she beamed at the camera, secure in the love of her parents. This was before Daddy disappeared—before the absence that sent her life into chaos.

There were a few photographs from their home in Marietta. Her father must have gotten a camera at some point, but the candid pictures stopped abruptly after Daddy's disappearance.

"Finding much?" Janice came over and stood next to LuAnn.

"There aren't a lot of pictures from when I was a kid," LuAnn said.

"Photography was quite expensive back then," Janice said. "We forget that now, with cameras in our phones and everywhere we look. Most people didn't have cameras, and even if you did, film was expensive to buy and develop."

"So no selfies," LuAnn said. "Actually, that sounds kind of lovely to think about."

Janice laughed. "Are there any pictures from family gatherings? Or church picnics? Or anything like that?"

"Not that I'm coming across," LuAnn said. "But then, you're right about the cost, and once Daddy left, there really wasn't much to spare."

"You make it sound like he packed up and left of his own volition," Janice said. "You know he only left because he had to. He never would have left if he'd had the choice."

"I know," LuAnn said. "I do know that. But after a lifetime of believing otherwise, it's still hard to think about it like that."

LuAnn did know now how hard it had been for him to leave, and that he'd only done so to keep his family safe. But for so many years, she had felt abandoned by her father, and those feelings drove some of the poor decisions she'd made when it came to men. Not Jesse—he'd been the first good man she'd loved. But the man before him—he'd been married, and after she found out, LuAnn had had to admit that the signs were there. She'd overlooked them because she'd wanted so badly to be loved.

"Look how cute you were," Janice said, pointing to a school photo of LuAnn from the second grade. "This must have been after you left Marietta. And you think Jay is from after Marietta, right?"

LuAnn nodded. The accent, the nickname, the mining reference—all of it pointed to a connection to LuAnn from her time in West Virginia as a girl. "If he was from Marietta, why would he come here on a tour, especially if he didn't want anyone to know about his connection to the place?"

LuAnn flipped through the remainder of the books, enjoying pictures from her life and her mother's life, but nothing stood out to her. She didn't know what she'd been hoping for, really—some lighted arrow, maybe, pointing toward the person she was supposed to investigate. But the feeling that she was missing something, that niggling feeling that the answer was right there, if she could only see it, was back, stronger than ever.

LuAnn's phone rang, pulling her out of her reverie. She reached for it and glanced at the screen. Brad.

"Hi there," she said as she put the phone to her ear.

"Hi. I just wanted to check and see how it's going. Did Mark and Lauren get there all right?"

"Yes, they got here this afternoon, and they're off exploring the town. Ethan too. He seems like a nice kid."

"Sure. He's nice." Somehow, the way Brad said it, it almost sounded like an insult.

"He seemed really great, actually," LuAnn said. "I think you may be a bit too hard on him."

Brad sighed. "LuAnn, please don't take this the wrong way," he started. LuAnn immediately felt certain she wasn't going to like whatever came next. "But you only met him briefly. Of course he seems nice. I've never doubted his politeness. That's not the issue."

"I'm just saying, maybe it's worth giving him a chance."

Brad was quiet for a minute, and then he said, "You know, I need to get going. Are we still on for a meeting with Lauren and Ethan to go over the details tomorrow at two?"

LuAnn paused to gather her thoughts. "Yes, that's great." She tried to keep herself from sounding as wounded as she felt. "I'll see you here then."

"Great. I'll talk to you then." He hung up, and LuAnn ended up staring down at her suddenly silent phone. That was abrupt. She and Brad didn't talk every night, but when they did, it was usually a rather lengthy conversation. But just now he'd gotten off the phone right after she'd mentioned giving Ethan a chance. Could he really be upset at her about that? Or was she just reading into it something that wasn't there?

"Everything okay?" Janice asked her from the stove. She'd gone back to cooking dinner.

"Yes, I think so," LuAnn said. No sense worrying about this now. She'd see Brad tomorrow, and hopefully they could smooth it all out then.

"Would you like some dinner?"

LuAnn joined Janice at the table, and as they ate they talked over what she'd learned by looking at the pictures, which was a big fat nothing, as far as LuAnn was concerned.

Janice took her plate to the sink. "What's in that other bin you brought home?" she asked.

"Oh, just some old home movies I took when I was in high school."

"You took home movies?" Janice's eyebrows shot up.

"They weren't very good." LuAnn laughed. "I wanted to be a movie star, and I thought practicing in front of the camera would help."

"But where did you get a camera?"

"I saved up my tips from the diner and bought it used from the high school. They gave me a good deal."

"That's pretty impressive," Janice said. "So what's on the film?"

"I don't know," LuAnn said. "I think it's mostly me prancing around in front of the camera, unfortunately."

"Well let's see it."

LuAnn looked around the room. If she set up the projector on the coffee table and took down the painting on the far wall, she could probably project it there.

"Let me see if I still remember how to do this," she said, rising. She went into her bedroom and retrieved the box and then spent the next few minutes trying to remember how to thread the narrow strip of brittle film through the projector. Janice lifted the painting off its hook and set it to the side, and a few minutes later, LuAnn flipped the switch and the film began playing. LuAnn laughed and Janice clapped her hands as the flickering frames showed fourteen-year-old LuAnn dancing on a picnic bench in the backyard.

"Look at you!" Janice said. LuAnn had been thin, almost wiry, and her wavy hair bounced around her shoulders as she danced to some long-forgotten song.

"I was ready for the big screen, don't you think?" LuAnn laughed. She'd certainly thought so at the time. She had been ready to buy her ticket to Hollywood. Looking back now, she wondered how much of that had been genuine interest in acting and how much she had simply seen it as her ticket out of West Virginia. In any case, by the time she'd gotten old enough for it to matter, she'd settled on college as a more promising career path.

"That was fun." Janice clapped as the film ended, the plastic strip whipping around the reel. "Let's see another."

LuAnn took the film spool off the projector and set another one in its place. "Isn't it funny how much technology has advanced in such a short time?" she said as a video she'd shot inside the diner played on the screen. Eleanor waved to the camera, her familiar apron tied around her waist, a coffeepot in her hand. "Today you could shoot a much better quality video on your phone and play it back instantly."

"It's amazing," Janice said, nodding at the screen. "Is that your mom?"

LuAnn smiled as the camera turned, and her mother appeared on the screen. She had a tray of food perched on her shoulder, and she waved the camera away with her free hand. LuAnn tried to swallow but couldn't. There she was. It was amazing to see her like that, just as LuAnn remembered her. She watched, with tears in her eyes, until the movie cut off.

"That was the diner, huh?"

LuAnn nodded. She'd talked about the diner many times, but her friends had never seen it before. She cleared her throat. "It sure was."

"It's fun to see it," Janice said, turning to look back at the box of film spools. "What else is in there?"

"Let's do one more," LuAnn said. She didn't want to hold Janice hostage all night. She threaded another reel onto the projector. A moment later, a room full of people around a table filled the screen. Her grandmother Marie was at the end of the table bending over a cake with one lit candle. A paper birthday hat was perched on her head at an angle, and she was surrounded by children and teenagers.

"This was Grams's sixtieth birthday," LuAnn recalled. "We all went to her house to celebrate."

"Who are the other people?" Janice asked.

"Those are my cousins. That's Kathy there on the left." She pointed to a girl with curly hair wearing a too-small knee-length dress. "She's a few years older than I am. She's Elmer's daughter. Next to her is Eric. He's probably eight or so. That's my aunt Barbara's boy. And the little ones to the right are Denise, John, and Pete. Jack's kids. I still keep in touch with Denise." After a moment, she added, "Jack died in a mining accident when I was thirteen or fourteen, so this must be shortly after that."

"Yikes." Janice took a deep breath. "That's awful. With three kids?"

"It was terrible," LuAnn confirmed, watching the faces of her cousins as they sang for Grams. "It was a huge accident, actually. An explosion deep down in the mine. Dozens of miners died. It devastated the town, which was pretty much all centered on mining."

"How horrible," Janice said. "All those men, killed, just like that?"

"Just like that," LuAnn confirmed. Though LuAnn and her mother had lived an hour away, and she hadn't seen the aftermath of the explosion firsthand, all her life she'd heard about the accident and how it had affected her family and the small town they'd come from. "There were so many children without fathers suddenly. So many lives destroyed."

But even as she talked about it, even as she watched her cousins' faces on the screen, that something was niggling at the back of LuAnn's mind. Something that was there, just out of reach.

"What is it?" Janice asked. "I can see you're puzzling over something."

"I'm not sure," LuAnn said, but when the film ended, she rewound it and started it over. She watched it again, studying the faces of her small cousins. When it was over the second time, she respooled the film and set it in the box.

"You're thinking about something," Janice said.

LuAnn didn't answer for a minute. She was going through scenarios in her head, trying to connect the dots, grasping at whatever it was that was just out of reach.

"I think I need to call my cousin Denise."

CHAPTER EIGHTEEN

LuAnn pulled off the highway and turned onto a country road just outside of Fairmont, West Virginia. She'd never been to Denise's house before, but she'd sent Christmas cards and seen posts on Facebook when Denise and her husband, Jim, bought the house, so she knew it was on a narrow road that threaded past cornfields and over hills. She followed the directions on her phone screen and drove past stately old homes on plots next to run-down trailers, all surrounded by gorgeous rolling green hills. A few minutes later, she pulled into the driveway of Denise's two-story home perched on top of a hill and surrounded by green lawn. It was only a few years old, with dormer windows on the second floor and a wide front porch.

LuAnn turned off the engine and sat in her car for a moment, trying to gather the courage to go to the door. When she'd called Denise last night, Denise had been surprised to hear from her but invited her to come over this morning to chat. The tour group was checking out before their ghost tour this afternoon. They would need to turn the rooms over quickly so the wedding guests could check in, but the meeting with Brad and Lauren to go over the wedding details wasn't until two, so LuAnn decided she had time. She'd been surprised during the two-hour drive from Marietta by the way the hilly roads and the farms and the cabins tucked under trees next to the rivers had unearthed old memories. Something about the landscape of your childhood never really left you, she thought, and seeing it made the memories come rushing back. Traveling these back roads to visit her grandparents in their little house over by the creek. The year the creek had flooded, and they'd all spent days cleaning and airing out the basement. The joy of gatherings with her cousins, especially after her father disappeared, and family had felt especially fragile.

LuAnn pushed open her car door and took a deep breath. She didn't need to be afraid, she reminded herself. This was her cousin. Denise had always been friendly and welcoming, and she'd sounded happy to hear from LuAnn. But that didn't mean she was going to want to answer the questions LuAnn had come here to ask. LuAnn walked to the door, rang the doorbell, and listened as it echoed inside. Denise had done well for herself. She'd married a local dentist and worked in an administrative office at the nearby university, and she'd come a long way from the dingy trailer where she'd grown up after her father died.

"Hello!" The door opened, and Denise wrapped LuAnn in a big hug. "Oh, my goodness. It's so good to see you!"

Denise still had the same curly hair and the same wide smile.

"It's good to see you too," LuAnn said. "This place is gorgeous."

"Thank you." Denise smiled and gestured for LuAnn to come inside. A little dog ran in from the kitchen and started yapping. "Hush, Milo," Denise said, scooping him up. "We're still working on making it exactly the way we want it, but it's coming along. We spend most of our weekends driving to football camps and hockey tournaments, so we don't have as much time to work on it as we'd like."

"It's beautiful," LuAnn said. "How are the kids, aside from having to drive them all over the state for sports?"

"They're good. Tyler is going to be a freshman at WVU, if you can believe it. He wants to study engineering."

"That's impressive."

"We'll see how it goes. He's planning to play football, so I suspect he's mostly interested in studying weight rooms and parties. But he's doing great." Denise led LuAnn into the living room and gestured for her to sit on one of the two tan couches oriented toward a large flat-screen television. "And Ryan is going to be a junior at the high school. He's really into marching band and orchestra."

"That's wonderful." The room was comfortable, with big windows letting in light and walls painted a soft beige. On the wall behind the couch, black metal letters spelled out *Home is wherever I'm with you.* "And how are you doing?"

"Oh, you know. It's summertime, so that's good. Work slows down, which is nice."

They chatted for a while about the family vacation they were planning later in the summer and Michael's dental practice, and LuAnn asked about Denise's brothers, John, who worked at the post office down the road, and Pete, who was a large-animal veterinarian. Denise wanted to hear all about the inn and what it was like to run a hotel. Then Denise said, "So. You mentioned you had questions about Daddy."

"Yes." LuAnn cleared her throat, trying to figure out the best way to phrase her question. "I was wondering if you could tell me about the mining accident. I remember when it happened, but you know how teenagers are. I didn't pay as much attention as I probably should have." On the phone, LuAnn had just hinted that she was interested in gathering family history, but she hadn't told Denise why she was so interested in this mining accident specifically.

"It was terrible. I was just a kid, you know." The Farmington Mine Disaster had happened in November 1968; according to LuAnn's calculations, Denise had been five at the time. "So my memories aren't all that clear. But I remember being woken up because the house was shaking. I've never felt anything like it before or since. Maybe it's what an earthquake feels like, I don't know. I thought it was the Lord coming back at first, but then the long whistle blew."

"The long whistle meant there was something wrong?"

"The long whistle meant an emergency. Momma flew out of her bedroom and out of the house, and I ran out after her, of course, but it was dark—this was very early in the morning— and you couldn't see anything."

"That must have been frightening."

"It was terrible. People were running out of all the houses around us. Miners who were off duty at the time ran over to try to help, and those of us who had someone in the mine..." Her voice trailed off, and she took a deep breath. "It was such a small town you know, and everyone around us was affiliated with the mine. So it was just...Everyone was in a panic."

She paused for a moment, and then she continued.

"My momma yelled at me to keep an eye on the younger children, so I stayed put, but you could hear the screaming and the wailing, and soon you could smell the smoke even from where we lived."

LuAnn tried to imagine leaving a five-year-old in charge of her two younger siblings and began to understand how frightened Aunt Kelly must have been when she ran out of the house that morning.

"How long did it take until you knew what had happened?"

"Momma learned about the explosion pretty much right away, but she didn't say anything about it at first when she came back a few hours later. But she didn't need to. It was pretty clear what had happened down in the mine. By this time, the sun was up and you could see fire and smoke pouring out of the mine from the yard. I knew Daddy was working there at the time."

"That must have been scary."

"I tried to focus on keeping Pete calm. John was just a baby, you know, so he had no idea what was going on, but Pete was three, and he knew something was up."

LuAnn knew from her research last night that it had been a major explosion in the number nine mine, in the Llewellyn shaft, and that seventy-eight miners had died in the tragedy.

"How long was it before you got the news?"

"Like I said, Momma came home a while later to make sure we were okay, but she didn't know a lot then. There were men coming out from the mine, and no one knew whether the rest of them were going to make it out or not."

LuAnn had read that twenty-one men made it out after the explosion, but attempts to get the rest of the men out were thwarted by further explosions underground that day, and later, by methane gas that made it difficult for the rescue teams.

"We didn't know for sure about Daddy until the next week, when they said there was no one else left alive in the tunnel. It was a very sad Thanksgiving for the entire town."

LuAnn had read that once that determination had been made, they had cemented over the entrance to the mine to seal off the underground fires. But she had also read something else.

"I read that the bodies of several of the miners trapped in the tunnel that day were never recovered. And I have this vague memory…"

"That's right." Denise nodded. "Eventually, once they opened the tunnel back up again, they did find most of the men, but there were nineteen they never found, including Daddy." She was so calm, so composed, talking about this. LuAnn wasn't sure she would be able to remain so unaffected. "They say those men were the closest to the explosion, and they just burned right up. There was nothing left to find."

"And the service you had…?" LuAnn remembered a funeral in a small white church, remembered sitting uncomfortably in the wooden pews in a navy-blue dress, watching those around her cry.

"It was a memorial service. There was nothing to bury." And then, before LuAnn could ask, she added, "There's a little plot out at the cemetery, but there's nothing inside the casket."

"That must have been hard." It was at least some small comfort to LuAnn to know where her mother's final remains were, and to be able to visit her there.

"Yes, it was," Denise said. She was quiet for a moment, and then she shook her head.

"What?"

Denise laughed a little, hesitated. And then she said, "Grandma Monroe was the only one smiling in the church that day."

"What do you mean?" Grandma Monroe was Denise's mother's mother, and no relation to LuAnn, but she'd met her a few times.

"Oh, she never liked Daddy, that was clear even to me as a kid. Well, you know she wouldn't have said yes to the marriage in the first place except Momma was expecting. Seven months later, here I come." Denise gave a little wave with her hands. "She always wanted more for Momma than being a coal miner's wife. She never warmed up to Daddy."

It sounded harsh, and for Denise to have noticed even as a child, Grandma Monroe must not have done a very good job of hiding her disdain for her daughter's husband. But LuAnn thought back and wondered if there was more to it than Grandma Monroe just not liking him or not forgiving him for getting Aunt Kelly pregnant.

"What was he like?" LuAnn tried to ask it gently, abstractly, as if she had no memories of him herself. But she did. She hadn't known Uncle Jack well, but she remembered a volatile man, uninterested in those around him and disinclined to engage in conversation. She also remembered hints about his drinking, about squandering his paycheck at the local bar. She even remembered hearing her mother and her sister say that his death was a blessing in disguise, though even in retrospect she had a hard time seeing how that was possible. Could Mother have really said something like that about her younger brother? He'd had three little kids. Wasn't a volatile dad still better than no dad? But hadn't there been something about a payout from the mine, after the fact? A settlement of sorts?

"Well, I was just a kid, and you know how little girls idolize their dads." She pressed her lips together.

LuAnn tried to phrase this next bit carefully. "I remember hearing that he could be difficult."

"Mom and Dad fought a lot," Denise confirmed. "I don't think he ever hit her, but he did yell a lot, especially after he'd been drinking."

"So it wasn't a happy marriage?"

"No, I wouldn't say it was. She loved him, I do believe that. And at one point he must have loved her too. But it had to have been hard, with three little kids and the only job around being in a coal mine." She shook her head. "I mean, there's nothing wrong with mining, don't get me wrong. It's just that, well, Momma once told me that he'd never wanted that life. She said he'd had big dreams to travel the world, to go to college, to own a business. But he kind of got stuck here, and mining was what there was. But I guess she was trying to help me see that he would have had a different life if things hadn't quite happened the way they had."

"She meant the pregnancy?"

Denise nodded.

"That's quite a burden to put on a child." It wasn't Denise's fault she'd been conceived at an inconvenient time.

"She didn't mean it like that. I think she was trying to show me that there was more to him than the man I knew. That he was smart and ambitious and that my memories of him were not the whole man."

LuAnn nodded, and she thought for a moment. It all added up. If her burgeoning theory was right, it all made sense. He'd never wanted this life. He'd gotten stuck here and had a few kids and drank too much to try to forget, for a little while, the fact that he had intended to be someone else entirely.

Had he eventually realized his goal?

Chapter Nineteen

January 15, 1860

Jason found Prudence sitting on a kitchen chair, bent over the letter, a short while later.

"Is thee all right?" He rushed into the kitchen and crouched down next to her. He was no doubt concerned. Moses was crawling around the living room untended. The stove was cold. She had not yet started dinner, and she knew she needed to, but she could not summon the strength to stand. "What news did that letter contain?"

Prudence took a few deep breaths. She tried to calm herself, to work up the strength to say the words out loud.

"It was a letter from my aunt," she managed to say.

Jason glanced over at Moses and saw that he was okay, and then he dropped down into the chair beside her, his hand on her arm.

"The one in Hancock County," he said. "The one thee wrote to in the fall."

Prudence nodded. "She got my letter, and she wrote back."

Jason was nodding, and she realized he'd probably already understood that.

"She says she would have written years ago, but she did not know I was alive, and she had no idea where to find me. She never received the letters Anna sent her. She tells me..." She took a deep breath. "She tells me news of our family. Of those in our community."

Jason, ever patient, asked gently, "And what does she say?"

"She says..." Again, a long deep breath. "She says my mother is gone. Passed many years ago."

Jason didn't say anything, just wrapped his arm around her back, and she loved him for it. Most men would have felt the need to find words to make her feel better, but Jason understood that there was no fixing this. That even though she'd known somewhere deep in her gut, for years, even though she'd always assumed her mother was gone, it still hurt more than words could express to know for sure. They sat in quiet for a moment, but then Prudence found the words. "But she also said something else."

Jason sat still, waiting for her to say more.

"She tells me..." Prudence pressed her eyes closed, trying to make the words seem real. "She tells me that my father is alive. That he, too, is free, and that she knows where he is. She says that I can see my father again."

CHAPTER TWENTY

LuAnn ran her theory around in her mind the whole way home. It would have taken cunning and initiative, and it would have taken a man who was unhappy enough with his life to never look back. But the more she thought it through, the more it seemed to fit. If Uncle Jack had somehow *not* been in the mine that morning after all, if something had kept him from going inside when he was supposed to...If he'd seen the explosion and known that the men inside were goners...Could he really have done it? Could he really have simply walked away, knowing he'd be presumed dead? Could he have walked away from his wife and his three children in pursuit of a life that had slipped out of his grasp?

LuAnn wasn't sure how it would have worked, exactly. Had he reported for work as normal and been inside the mine but then come out for some reason before the explosion? Had he had a friend clock in for him while he slept off a hangover nearby? It was impossible to say. All LuAnn knew for sure was that Uncle Jack had been presumed to be in the mine that day, but his body had never been found.

She did the math in her head as she zoomed down the highway, ten over the speed limit. Jack had to be in his midseventies now. That would mean he was in his early twenties in

1968. That checked out. The first record of Jay they'd found had been when he'd joined the army in 1969. Was it possible? Had her uncle Jack simply walked away from the burning mine, adopted a new identity, and started a new life?

A slowdown on the highway meant that it was already almost two when LuAnn got back to the inn. The tour group had checked out, and Brad was waiting in the parlor with Janice and Tess when LuAnn came inside. Ethan sat across from him on the couch.

"Hello." Brad's face lit up when she came in. Order forms and invoices were spread out on the coffee table between them.

"Hi there. Sorry I'm late." LuAnn rushed in and closed the door behind her. She smiled at Brad, but she didn't have the same shivery feeling she usually felt when she saw him. She couldn't stop thinking about their last interaction, about how he'd shut down after she defended Ethan.

"You're just on time," Tess said. She gestured to the armchair across from her. "Have a seat. We were just going through some details with Brad and Ethan before the others get here."

"Where are Lauren and Mark?" LuAnn asked. If the meeting wasn't ready to start yet, was there time for her to run upstairs? She just needed to take a quick look at the photo album. She was almost sure that if she just glanced at it—

"They went wedding-dress shopping over at the outlet mall," Ethan explained.

LuAnn snapped back to the present, and she had to laugh. "Do you mean Lauren doesn't have a wedding dress picked out yet?"

"She kept saying she just wanted something simple. Something she'd be able to wear again." Ethan shrugged. "I have to admit, it makes a lot of sense to me."

"On her way out she told me she wasn't going to pick anything white," Janice said. "She wants something in a fun color."

"I hope she doesn't pick anything that clashes with the flowers," LuAnn said. She hadn't even considered the idea that the bride wouldn't be wearing white when they picked out the flowers. "She really is one of a kind, isn't she?"

"She really is," both Brad and Ethan said. And then Ethan laughed, while Brad gave the younger man a tight-lipped smile.

What was Brad's problem? LuAnn tried not to let it bother her. It wasn't her business. She didn't know their whole history, and it wasn't something she needed to get her hackles up about. But Ethan seemed like a nice guy and seemed to be totally in love with Lauren. Why couldn't Brad be happy for them?

Just then the door whooshed open, and Lauren came in, followed by her father. A white plastic garment bag was draped over Mark's arm.

"Looks like you found something," Janice said just a touch too cheerfully, trying to cover up the tension that hung in the air.

"We did. But I won't tell you a thing about it," Lauren said, closing the door behind her. "You'll just have to wait until Saturday to see it." She was looking at Ethan as she said it, and a goofy grin spread across his face.

"I'll go put this upstairs, and then we'll be ready to look at the plans," Mark said.

Once again, LuAnn considered just running upstairs. She would be back before Mark was, she would guess. And it would only take her a moment to check...

But Lauren was already settling in on the couch next to Ethan, and she was looking at them expectantly.

"Did your meeting with the pastor go well?" Tess asked.

"It went great. We have a quick rehearsal tomorrow night, after my brother and Lauren's best friend get into town," Ethan said. Which reminded LuAnn—they needed to turn those guest rooms over sooner rather than later, before Ethan's parents came in tonight. Well, there would be time, after she ran upstairs to check that album. She mentally kicked herself for not asking Denise if she had a more recent picture of her father than LuAnn had.

"How about we start with the menu, then," LuAnn said. "When your guests arrive after the service, we'll have hors d'oeuvres on the patio." She passed Lauren the list of canapés they had settled on—mac and cheese bites, mini sliders, meatballs on toothpicks.

"This looks perfect," Lauren said.

"I'm getting hungry just thinking about it," Ethan said. "I was so afraid it would be all fussy food I've never heard of, but this looks like food my friends will love."

LuAnn caught Tess's eye and held back a smile.

"And this is the menu for the buffet," LuAnn said, passing them a paper.

They went through the details of their plans for the reception, from the decorations to the food to the timing, and

Lauren enthusiastically approved all of their choices. Mark's only request was that they play music from the sixties during the reception—apparently he had a thing for the oldies, which LuAnn found delightfully charming. They promised to set up a dance floor under the trees. Lauren especially loved the photo booth idea and clapped her hands at the disposable cameras.

"You did such a great job, Uncle Brad," Lauren said. Brad's face filled with pride.

"This really does look incredible," Ethan said, looking around the room at the three innkeepers. "Thanks to all of you for pulling this together."

LuAnn wouldn't have noticed it if she hadn't already picked up on the animosity Brad had for Ethan. But in that moment, she saw something like disdain cross Brad's face. He covered it quickly, and she was sure that no one else noticed, but she was also sure that Brad's feelings about Ethan hadn't changed. But after watching them all interact, she thought she might have an inkling what was going on.

A few minutes later, Lauren and Ethan headed out to go try another ice cream shop. Mark was going to stay back to hang out with Brad. But while everyone was moving around, LuAnn pulled Brad aside. "Can I talk to you for a minute?"

"Sure." She sensed a tiny bit of hesitation, as if he knew what she wanted to talk about, but then he gamely followed her out onto the patio.

"I know you think I'm being too hard on Ethan," he said as he closed the glass-paned door behind them.

"It's not that, exactly," LuAnn said. "I mean, yes, that's it, but I wondered if it maybe has very little to do with Ethan."

"What do you mean?" He narrowed his eyes.

She had to tread carefully here. "It's obvious how much you adore Lauren," she said. "And I can see why. She's wonderful. She's smart and caring and funny and pretty, and she's grown into a lovely woman."

Brad waited for her to go on.

"But that's just it. She's a woman now. A grown adult. And she's old enough to make her own choice about who she wants to marry."

Brad didn't answer.

"I know you want to protect her, to make sure nothing hurts her—"

"I promised her mother on her deathbed that I would protect her," Brad said. "That I would look out for her, no matter what."

LuAnn nodded. "And you've done a wonderful job. But right now, I don't think she needs protecting. She loves Ethan, and he's crazy about her. He's kind and responsible, and he's a good guy. What she needs is for you to trust that she's made the right choice."

"She could have anyone," Brad said.

"And she's chosen Ethan." LuAnn took a tentative step forward. "And I don't honestly believe you would have been happier with any other choice. I think you don't really believe anyone is good enough for her. Don't get me wrong, that only shows how much you love her. But it also means you're not going to enjoy what should be one of the most important days of her life."

Brad was quiet for a moment. LuAnn held her breath.

He looked like he was going to say something.

And then, almost reluctantly, he shook his head, muttered, "You're way off base," and went back inside, leaving LuAnn standing alone on the patio.

LuAnn stood still for a moment, thinking back through the exchange. Had she approached it wrong? She no doubt had, she thought. She probably shouldn't have—

But then, if not her, who? He hadn't taken it well, that was clear. But was she off base with what she'd said? LuAnn thought back through it again and realized that no, she still believed what she'd said to him. His feelings about Ethan weren't really about Ethan. They were really about Lauren, the little girl he loved, growing up.

LuAnn shook her head. His reaction had hurt, there was no doubt about that. He'd never spoken to her like that before. But LuAnn couldn't sit here and dwell on it. She had something she needed to do, and the sooner she took care of it, the better. She turned and walked back into the inn. The lobby was empty, and she hurried up the stairs. The elevator would take too long. She was out of breath when she stepped into her bedroom, but she hurried over to the stack of photo albums on her desk and rummaged through them. The photo had been in—*there*. She grabbed the album with the white faux-leather cover, pulled it out, and flipped to the photo from her parents' wedding. There was the one she was thinking of—the one of her mother and father with Mom's family flanking the couple. There was Aunt Barbara, and Uncle Elmer, Uncle Donald, and...she picked up the album and studied Uncle Jack's face. He had been so young in this photo, no more than eight or nine, probably. He was gangly and awkward, and yet...And yet, there it was. He had changed so much in the intervening fifty years that LuAnn hadn't seen it before. And of course, she hadn't been looking, because after all Uncle Jack was supposed to be dead. But looking at this photo now, it became clear that all week when she had been chatting with Jay, she had really been talking to her uncle Jack.

LuAnn sat back and let the truth wash over her. He was alive. He hadn't died in the mine explosion after all. For whatever reason, Jack hadn't been in the mine that day, and after the explosion, he had realized his opportunity and simply walked away.

LuAnn couldn't even fathom it. All these years they had thought he was dead, and instead he'd simply just...vanished. Walked away from his wife, from his children, from his home and family. How could a person do that? *Why* would a person do that? Had things really been so bad at home that he'd simply decided to never see them again? And how could he have simply taken on another person's identity, another person's life?

LuAnn couldn't imagine what had been going through his head, what had motivated him. But she knew what kind of damage he had caused. His children had grown up without a father, in poverty, and that pain ran deep. Still to this day, they were marked by that loss. His wife had spent her entire life struggling, taking whatever jobs she could get and living wherever she could afford, trying to keep a roof over their children's heads. LuAnn remembered how she'd looked at the funeral—stunned, scared, and completely overwhelmed.

The funeral. LuAnn had been to Jack's funeral. And here he was, fifty years later, alive and well.

She tried to keep calm. She tried not to judge, not to assume she knew the whole story, to wait until she heard Jack's side of the story. But she couldn't stop the feelings of anger, betrayal, and righteous indignation that rose up in her. It had been selfish, pure and simple. It had been astoundingly self-centered and amazingly short-sighted. He had abandoned his children. He had married again, when he *already had a wife*. He had shirked his responsibilities and taken on an easier life, a happier life. No more coal mines and trailers full of children; Jack had gotten himself a new life, one with country clubs and golf outings and a big house with columns.

She was glad the tour group was gone so she didn't have to look at him, to know what he'd done, to have to pretend that she didn't know. He had obviously realized who she was from the beginning, and he hadn't said a thing. He had let her believe—he'd let them all believe...She shook her head. She never wanted to see him again.

And yet, LuAnn couldn't help thinking, he was her uncle. Her flesh and blood. Now that her mother was gone, he was the last link to that generation of her family. And now that she knew, she couldn't exactly keep this quiet. Denise and her brothers had to know. They had to know that their father had come back from the dead.

She didn't want to face him, to confront him with what she knew. But could she really just let him leave town without seeing him again? She had his address, she reasoned, and she knew where to find him. But he was probably still here. The tour group had been planning to attend a ghost tour of Marietta before they got on the bus and headed to the next stop on the tour. She glanced at her clock and checked the time. It was just after three now. Hadn't the tour started at two? He was still here, she thought. She still had time to catch him, to confront him, if she wanted to. But even as she was thinking it, she knew what she was going to do. LuAnn had never been content to let a mystery remain unsolved. She knew the truth; now she had to tell the truth, and see what Jay—Uncle Jack— had to say.

LuAnn gathered her purse and tucked her phone into it, and then she headed downstairs. The lobby was quiet. She looked around and saw Tess and Janice on the lawn under the trees, no doubt arranging tables in their minds. She could just pop out and tell them where she was going, but now that she was on her way, she was frustrated with the very idea of stopping and taking the time to explain what she'd discovered. She had to catch Jay before the tour group left town. She had to confront him with the truth and see what he had to say for himself. She grabbed a notebook from the desk drawer and scribbled a quick note—*Going to ghost tour to confront Jay, be back soon*—and left it on the desk, and then she ran out to her car.

When Meaghan had shown her the itinerary for the ghost tour, she'd seen that it ended at the Lafayette Hotel. That made sense, she supposed. It was the most famous of the hotels in town, named after the Marquis de Lafayette, the French hero of the American Revolution, who visited the town in 1825. It was also home to some of Marietta's most well-known ghost stories. There were rumors that an old owner haunted the upper floors of the hotel, as well as stories of pianos playing themselves and cleaning staff and guests seeing mysterious apparitions and nonsense like that. If the tour group hadn't gotten to the hotel by now, they would soon, she reasoned. She started the car and headed that way.

In her pettiest moments, LuAnn considered the Lafayette—one of the oldest and most expensive hotels in town—their competition, but she had to admit that it was a grand old place with a rich history, and the building itself was stunning. The hotel's distinctive triangular shape with its rounded front was beautiful, and the brick and stone façade was tasteful and imposing. The hotel overlooked the river, and she had to imagine that some of the guest rooms had stunning views. LuAnn saw the tour bus along the street when she pulled up. She parked and hurried inside and across the carpeted lobby. The woodwork was beautiful gleaming maple, and the walls were painted a creamy yellow, with gorgeous green and red trim. The coffered ceiling added a dramatic touch, and the furniture was all reproductions of the Victorian era, with its tufted settees and brocade armchairs. Even the elevator doors were paneled with rich maple so they blended in with the rest of the décor. Under normal circumstances, LuAnn would have been thrilled to stroll through the lobby and take in the atmosphere and maybe pick up an idea or two they could replicate in their own inn. But today, she was on a mission. She had practiced this on the way over.

"Hello," she said to the man behind the counter. He wore a starched white shirt under a reddish vest and smiled as she approached.

"Welcome to the Lafayette Hotel," he said. "Are you checking in?"

"Actually, I'm not," LuAnn said. "I'm trying to get an urgent message to the member of a group that I believe is on a tour at the moment."

"Ah." The man nodded. "The ghost tour?"

"Exactly. Are they here?"

"Yes, the group is touring the basement at the moment. What is the guest's name? I can send someone down to pass along a message."

LuAnn knew she should accept this. It's what they would have done at Wayfarers Inn. You couldn't have random people barging in and let them wander all over the hotel, no matter who they claimed they needed to see. Or she could simply wait by the bus. They'd head there after the tour, and LuAnn could stop Jay on the way. But she didn't want to mess up the entire group's schedule by delaying them. She wanted to talk to Jay privately, before the end of the tour. Besides, now that she knew the truth, she couldn't stand the thought of waiting to ask him what had really happened. To confront him with the truth. To demand answers.

"Actually, I would really like to go down and talk with him right away," she said.

"One moment, please. Let me see what I can do." The man smiled and turned to pick up the phone on the desk. While his shoulder was half-turned, LuAnn saw her opportunity. She'd noticed the door next to the elevators as she walked in. Those were the stairs to the basement, she knew. Janice had had a friend, Leslie, who worked in the business office and had shown them around when they were still trying to get the inn up and running. LuAnn remembered that this area was typically off limits to guests, but Leslie had taken them down and shown them the laundry facilities to give them an idea of the scale of the machines they would need to install in their own basement. Leslie had also mentioned rumors of a ghost that sometimes haunted the area near where the laundry was now, and LuAnn was pretty sure she could find the area again.

She causally walked toward the door, as if she were just wandering, and while she heard the man at the desk explaining the situation, she simply opened the door and ducked inside.

"Excuse me!" the man called, but instead of stopping, she hurried down the steps. LuAnn felt a thrill go through her as she bounded down the carpet-covered stairs, clutching the handrail. This was naughty, and a bit silly, but with every second, she was one step closer to getting to the truth. Jay would not be able to get out of Marietta without admitting to her what he'd done.

LuAnn paused at the bottom of the steps and then turned right, toward where she knew the laundry facilities were located—and where the ghost tour was most likely to be gathered. She heard the man from upstairs following her on the steps, so she opened the first door she saw—a supply closet, as it turned out—and ducked inside. Tiny bottles of shampoo and individually wrapped soaps and toothbrushes surrounded her. She waited until she heard him pass by, and then she waited a few minutes more, until he passed by going the other way, saying something into a walkie-talkie, and then she heard him go up the stairs. Then, slowly, she poked her head out. The coast was clear. She waited another minute, just to make sure, then stepped into the hall and turned toward the laundry area.

She heard the group before she saw them—heard the voice of the perky tour guide bouncing off the cement hallway. LuAnn turned the corner and there they were—all eight of them, plus Meaghan, listening as the young woman in a Ghost Tours of Marietta T-shirt told stories of workers hearing noises in empty rooms and seeing mysterious apparitions as they worked alone down here late at night. None of them noticed her, and she listened for a moment. The guide was a good storyteller. She almost made it sound plausible—almost. It was all ridiculous, obviously. Stories made up to lure tourists in. As Meaghan had said, people loved the idea of ghosts and unexplained phenomena. None of it was real, LuAnn knew. But still, down here in this dank basement, with its low ceiling and flickering lights, she could almost believe it.

"Could it be the ghost of Mr. Hoag roaming the halls of the hotel he gave his life to?" the chirpy tour guide was saying. "We may never know for sure." With that dramatic flourish, she turned and gestured for the group to follow her down the hallway toward another set of stairs. LuAnn followed behind and waited as Meaghan went up first, followed by Robert and Lisa. Jay and Jacqueline were toward the back of the group, Jay wearing that same straw hat. They were all headed upstairs, and LuAnn realized she was going to miss her opportunity.

"Jay," she called.

Jay's head whipped around, and his mouth fell open when he saw her there.

"Oh hi, LuAnn!" Jacqueline waved. "What a surprise to see you here. Have you been on the tour this whole time? My goodness, wasn't that fun?" She was starting up the stairs, talking the whole time.

"Can I speak with you for a moment?" LuAnn said to Jay.

He knew. Something in his face said he knew that she'd figured it out. His eyes were darting from side to side, looking for a way out. "I'm afraid we don't have time to chat right now," he said. He gestured toward the stairs, where the rest of the group was walking up. He stood on the second step. "It's time to get on the bus and head to the next town."

"They'll wait," LuAnn said. "This is important."

"I'm afraid I—"

"I want the truth, Jack."

He flinched at the sound of the name, but didn't say anything.

"Jay, are you coming?" Jacqueline called from the top of the stairs.

215

"I'll be right there," Jay called back. Jacqueline mumbled something under her breath and went the rest of the way up the steps. The heavy door closed behind her, and then they were alone in the basement. LuAnn knew she only had a few minutes, that the security team would no doubt be back to look for her, and that Jacqueline or Meaghan or someone else from the tour would come to search for Jay if he dawdled for more than a few minutes.

"They thought you were dead," LuAnn said. "We all thought you were dead. All these years, your family has been mourning you, and you were off living another life."

"You're mistaken," he said. His jaw moved up and down, his chin quivering just a bit. "You must be thinking of someone else."

"No, I'm not." LuAnn stepped toward him. "And I want answers. I want to know why you weren't in the mine that day. I want to know what happened to you. I want to know where you've been, why you left. Whether you ever looked back, whether you ever thought about the wife and kids you left behind. The kids who grew up without a father and missed you every single day of their lives."

The only thing that moved was a little muscle in his jaw. Otherwise, he stood still, watching her, his breath coming out in jagged little gasps. For a moment, LuAnn saw her mother in his features and knew that she'd finally found what had been nagging at her ever since she'd met him. He stepped slowly down one step, then the next.

"It was better that way," he finally said. "It was for the best."

It took LuAnn a moment to process what he'd said. He'd admitted it. But then, of course he had. He'd had no choice, she realized. He knew she knew.

"How could it possibly have been for the best?" LuAnn's voice echoed in the empty hallway. "How could it have been better for your kids to grow up without a father? To leave their mother without a way to make a living?" She took a small step toward him.

"There was a settlement," Jay said. "I knew if I was gone, if they thought I'd been killed, they would at least get that." He pulled the hat off his head and ran his fingers through his hair. "I was a terrible father. They were better off without me."

Based on what Denise had said and the rumors she'd heard when she was young, she had no doubt about the first part. But she didn't believe the second part, not for a moment.

"No, they weren't," LuAnn said. "And Aunt Kelly wasn't either."

"I don't know." His hair was now sticking up on one side, and he held his hat in his hand. "Things were...It was tough. It was a bad time. You were just a kid back then. You didn't understand how bad things really were."

LuAnn had understood plenty, even then, but she wanted to hear it from him. "Bad how?" She cocked her head. "At the mine?"

"At the mine. At home. It was just..." He looked down at the floor. "We were poor. We were young. We had too many kids. I—I drank too much." He shook his head. "I didn't plan

217

it. You have to understand. I never intended to…I never intended any of it."

She wanted to say something but waited for him to go on.

"I couldn't believe it when I saw you," Jay said. Something in his voice was softening, losing the raw edge that had been there when she'd first stopped him. "I recognized you right away. But I knew you didn't know me."

"I thought you'd died fifty years ago," LuAnn said. "It never occurred to me that I would ever see you alive again."

He smiled ruefully. "I'm like a bad penny that way, I guess."

"You denied that we knew each other."

"I couldn't exactly tell you the truth, now could I? Not with my wife right there."

"She doesn't know."

"Of course not." He looked like he wanted to say more, but then he took a breath and grasped the handrail. "How did you figure it out, in the end?" He seemed to struggle to come up with the words.

"I put it together slowly," LuAnn said. "And this morning I talked to Denise. That's when I knew for sure."

A look she couldn't read passed over his face at the mention of his daughter's name.

"You always were a smart one," he said, shaking his head. And then, almost as an afterthought, he added, "I just thought, better to have them believe I'd died at work than know the truth."

Had he really believed that? LuAnn couldn't say if that was what he'd honestly believed at the time or whether that was a story he told himself now, even all these years later, to justify what he'd done.

"What was the truth?" LuAnn asked. "Where were you that day? Why weren't you there?"

He waited a moment, but then he answered, "I was with a woman. A— Well, it doesn't matter now. In any case, I was running late for work because I was with someone other than my wife." The words sounded hollow, like the part of him that had appeared a moment ago had vanished. "I was on my way to the mine, you understand. And my buddy and I, we had a system where we'd clock in for each other if one of us was...running a bit late. Well, anyway. You could feel the explosion for miles. I ran toward the mine, but I was still half a mile away when I saw the flames shooting out, the smoke billowing up to the heavens." He shuddered. "I knew it was bad. I knew there would be dozens dead. And I knew they would all think I'd been inside. And I thought about how unhappy Kelly was, all the time. I thought about how often I came staggering home and how the kids were scared of me, how they would be better off with me gone. At least they'd get the settlement, and Kelly could start a new life. Marry someone who treated her well. Someone who would take care of her and the kids."

But *you* could have become that man, LuAnn wanted to insist. Jack could have left the drinking and the other women behind and become the man his wife and children deserved. After all, he'd done just that, hadn't he? Jacqueline obviously loved her husband, and Patrick and Mary Grace didn't have a violent drunk for a father. "So you saw the explosion and took your chance?"

"I genuinely thought it would be better that way. For everyone." He shrugged. "So I turned around and left. It was the simplest thing in the world, in the end. I turned around, walked away, and didn't look back."

"And you took someone else's identity."

"I needed a Social Security number." He shrugged, as if that absolved him for taking on someone else's life. "I figured joining the army was the best way to get out of Dodge, but I needed a Social Security number to do that."

"Did you know him?" LuAnn asked.

"No. I read about him in the paper. Did some research."

"But you only got away with it because there was a fire—" But even as she said the words, the look on his face changed. Hardened.

Goose bumps raised on her arms.

"The fire..."

At first he didn't say anything. He grasped the railing tightly, and then let it go. Then, finally, he answered. "I only did what I had to do."

She sucked in a breath. Up until this point, it had been possible to believe that he'd been a victim of sorts in all this as well. Sure, he'd done something terrible in abandoning his family, but circumstances had driven him to it. But now, hearing his confession that he'd done what he had to do, LuAnn began to get a prickling sensation at the back of her neck. He'd set the fire that had destroyed all the records.

He hadn't killed Jay Carroll, she reminded herself. Just taken advantage of the opportunity when he died. And he hadn't caused that explosion in the mine. They'd long ago determined that faulty ventilation and a disabled safety alarm had been the cause of the disaster. He wasn't that evil. But the prickling sensation stayed.

"It's like a miracle," she said, a bit too brightly. "To have you back after all this time. And like I said, I spoke with Denise this morning. She and John and Pete will be—"

"Oh, they can't find out," Jack said. His voice was quiet, but it sounded like gravel. Rough, sharp.

"But of course they'll want to—"

"No. They won't find out," Jack said. "No one will."

Was he asking her to keep a secret like this? LuAnn wasn't sure she could do that. But then his features hardened, and his eyes turned steely, and she began to understand that that wasn't what he intended at all.

"I'm old. I've made some mistakes, sure, but I've worked hard, and I'm not about to let it be taken away from me now. It would kill Jacqueline, and it would ruin Patrick's and Mary Grace's lives."

There was a cold feeling of dread in LuAnn's stomach, and she realized she was alone in the basement with him. She needed to get out of here. Where was that security team? Weren't they coming to look for her? She craned her neck to look behind her, but nothing moved in the hall.

"Why don't we go upstairs and talk about this," she said and moved toward the stairs. But Jack was still holding the handrail and stepped over so he blocked the stairs.

He couldn't possibly mean that he—but then, it sure seemed like he did.

Sure, this was her uncle. Her own flesh and blood. But he'd just admitted to a huge secret, one that could ruin everything about his pleasant life. What would he do to keep that secret?

"Uncle Jack." LuAnn tried appealing to his familial side. "I think if we just go up the stairs and talk about this, we can find a way forward that makes sense for all of us."

He didn't say anything. LuAnn started to brush past him, but he moved so he was completely blocking the stairs. She could see the runner's strength that had made her believe he could be behind the wallet theft. She turned to run down the hall to the other stairway.

"I don't want to do this," he said, reaching out and grabbing her wrist.

"You don't have to do anything," LuAnn said. What was he going to do? "We can just go upstairs—"

"Don't you see that we can't do that?" he hissed. LuAnn pulled back like she'd touched something hot, but he still had her wrist. His voice echoed in the empty corridor. "I tried to keep you out of this. I told you I didn't know you. But you kept pushing, and you kept digging. And now look where it's gotten us."

"We can just go—"

"You're not going anywhere." He lunged forward, and before she understood what was happening, he was dragging her down the hallway. "I didn't want to do this, Lulu, but you leave me no choice."

She recognized the words of a man who was used to blaming other people for his mistakes. Who didn't accept responsibility for his actions. That lined up perfectly with everything she knew about him so far—a man who had found his life and family too difficult and simply walked away.

She thought all this as he dragged her down the hallway and yanked open a closet door. A supply closet, but a different one than the one she'd hidden in. She could see it had bottles of bleach and cleaning chemicals lined up along the shelves and a line of buckets and mops along one wall.

"I told you to stop asking questions," he said. His voice broke a little on the last few syllables, and then he looked at her for a moment. In the dim light, she saw that his eyes were wide, his mouth open, his look...detached, somehow. It was almost as if the quiet, dapper man who had spent the last few days at their inn was gone entirely, replaced by...well, replaced by someone she didn't recognize. "See what you made me do?"

And with that, he shoved her into the closet and slammed the door shut. The force of his shove drove LuAnn to her hands and knees, and she hit her head on something. She felt a stabbing pain, and dizziness overtook her in the darkness. It was a few moments before she was able to get to her feet and look for the light switch, and even then, she was shaking. She ran her hand over the wall near the door, found the switch, and felt a small measure of relief when the dim fluorescent light flickered on. Then she reached for the door handle. There was no lock on the inside, and he wouldn't have been able to—but when she pushed on the door, it didn't open. She tried again, this time using the weight of her body to shove against the door. It didn't budge. The handle turned, but the door was stuck shut. Had he jammed it somehow? Did the door lock automatically? But if it did, how had he opened it in the first place? LuAnn wasn't sure. All she knew was that when she tried the door handle, it turned, but the door wouldn't open.

LuAnn tried to stay calm. She would just call for help. She looked around the room. There was no phone in here. She pulled out her cell phone and looked at the screen. *No service*, it said in the top left corner. What? No! This wasn't possible. She walked around the small space, hoping to find a pocket where there was service, but found none. It must be the thick walls of the basement, she thought with a sigh. She tried to stay calm and took a long, deep breath. Someone would come down here soon. This was an active hotel. There was cleaning staff everywhere. Someone would come.

"Help," she called, banging on the door. "Help! Please let me out!" She yelled until her throat was hoarse, until her hands were bruised from pounding on the door, but there was no answer. Finally, she moved away from the door and sat down to wait.

Someone would come, she thought. They would need cleaning supplies soon. And she'd left that note for Tess and Janice. But would they be able to make sense of it? She thought back to what she'd written. Why hadn't she been more specific? Still, someone would come. The man at the front desk knew she'd gone down the steps. He knew she was down here.

But he hadn't come back to find her, she realized. She'd assumed he'd be back right away, but where was he?

Every minute that passed seemed to take forever. And this room smelled awful. Under the sharp bite of chemicals, there was the underlying smell of damp and iron and—she took in a few breaths. It was more sulfurous. She wrinkled her nose.

Why hadn't she just waited to talk to Jay upstairs? Why had she rushed down here like an idiot? She had been so excited, so eager to confront him, and had ended up here. LuAnn lowered herself down to the ground and sat on the cold cement floor. She'd never expected something like this. He was her uncle; he'd been a guest in her family's home. It had never occurred to her that he would lock her in a closet in the basement. She'd never imagined he would be the kind of person...

But then, why wouldn't he be, she realized. He was the kind of person who had walked away from his wife and children, letting them believe he was dead, for more than fifty years. Who had taken on a dead man's identity and burned down a funeral home to make sure no one ever found out. He'd built himself a nice life. Why wouldn't he lock his niece in a basement closet to protect his secrets? On the other hand, what did he accomplish by this, in the long run? She would just tell Denise and the boys when she got out. She would also write to Jacqueline and tell her. He was just delaying the inevitable. How could he not know that?

It was so quiet down here. She tried not to let her mind drift to the tour she'd just caught the end of. The one where the tour guide had explained that ghosts haunted these passageways. LuAnn knew everything along this part of the river had been underwater more than once when the Ohio had overflowed its banks, including the infamous flood of 1913.

Hundreds of people had died in that flood. Had any of them been in this basement? She shivered.

And the flood wasn't the only disaster this hotel had survived. There had been a fire, she thought. A fire that had completely destroyed the Bellevue Hotel, which had been the predecessor to the Lafayette on this spot. Many people had died in that fire, she remembered. In fact, at least one of the ghosts that had no doubt been mentioned on that ghost tour was a person who had been killed in the big fire.

There is no such thing as ghosts, she reminded herself. *Ghosts are not real.*

Ghosts were not real, but was she imagining the smell of...She took another breath. Was that smoke?

She was imagining it, surely. But then, the smell was getting stronger. He wouldn't have—but he had before. Although no one had been hurt when the funeral home burned down. He couldn't have set a fire knowing she was trapped down here. *Could he?*

How far would Jay go to protect his secret? With every second that passed, the smell of smoke grew more intense, and she realized she had her answer. Jay—her own uncle Jack—was willing to kill her to protect his secret.

LuAnn was back up, pounding on the door, shouting, trying to shove the door open with her shoulder, but it didn't budge. She almost jumped out of her skin when a piercing shriek tore through the basement, and she realized it was the fire alarm.

She tried not to panic. She tried to take long, deep breaths. People wouldn't just abandon the building now—

that man at the front desk knew she'd come down here. Surely someone—

But he would probably think she'd set the fire, she realized with a sad, sinking sense of inevitability. He would think she was long gone. There was no way he would come down into a burning basement to search for her.

Oh Lord, she prayed. *Please be near to me. Please help me.*

After six decades in church, LuAnn should have been more articulate, but now, as she was seeing the end of her life coming quicker with every second, it was all she could make herself say. *Oh Lord, please be near.*

No one was coming for her, she realized. No one was going to throw open that door. No one knew she was here.

And, she realized with a sad sigh, she was in a closet surrounded by flammable chemicals. *Oh Lord, please be near.*

LuAnn didn't know what to do. She couldn't just sit down and wait for death.

Well, she did know she had to get down low, she realized. Wasn't that what they said? Smoke rises, so stay along the floor. She crouched down and placed the hem of her shirt over her mouth. It would help for a little while. She thought about her mother, about how her mom had sacrificed everything to care for her. She missed her so deeply it hurt. *I guess I'll see you sooner than I expected, Mom.*

As she sat there, waiting for death to find her, she didn't have the words to express the fear, the gratitude, the hope that filled her heart. Instead, what came to her were the hymns she'd sung in that little white church in the hills of West Virginia.

"Blessed Assurance." "What a Friend We Have in Jesus." "Jesus Paid it All." "How Great Thou Art." "I'll Fly Away." "It is Well with My Soul." One after another, LuAnn sang the songs that had been the soundtrack to her childhood. She knew she shouldn't waste whatever oxygen there was left in here on singing, but then again she couldn't think of a better way to go out than singing praises to the Lord. At some point, the alarm stopped blaring. No doubt the system had been destroyed in the blaze. Surely she didn't have long left now.

And then, while she was on the third verse of "Amazing Grace," LuAnn heard something. Voices. Voices calling out. And then, could it really be? The sound of something scraping along the outside of the door. And then, just like that, the door was being yanked open. Janice and Tess stood in the doorway, flanked by two men in hotel uniforms. LuAnn recognized one of them as the man from the front desk.

"Are you all right?" Tess said, rushing into the closet.

"What happened?" Janice asked.

"The fire!" LuAnn hurried toward the door. "We have to get out, now!"

"It's okay," Tess said, reaching out for her.

"The fire is out." Janice was holding out her hands to stop LuAnn from running.

"But…what?" LuAnn looked from them to the hotel employees and back. And then she realized they were right. The hallway wasn't filled with smoke or flames. There was just a wet, smoky scent in the air.

"What happened?" she asked.

"The sprinklers took care of it," the man from the front desk said. She looked up. Water was still dripping from a fire sprinkler in the hallway.

Of course. The hotel might be historic, but the law would mandate that it have fire sprinklers. LuAnn wanted to laugh, but tears came out instead.

"Come on." Tess put her arm around LuAnn and pulled her into the hallway. "These men have a lot of questions, and you've got a lot of explaining to do."

LuAnn let herself be led out of the closet. She had a lot of questions too, but for now, she was just happy to be alive.

CHAPTER TWENTY-ONE

It wasn't until later that evening, after she'd repeatedly given her statement to the police and the hotel staff explaining how she'd ended up trapped in the burning basement, that she got the full story from Janice and Tess. How they'd wondered where she'd gone and finally found the note she'd left. How it had taken several phone calls to figure out where the ghost tour stopped and whether anyone had seen her at those stops. How, when they'd arrived at the Lafayette Hotel, they found the place evacuated and on fire.

"That's when we knew we'd found you," Tess said. "Classic LuAnn right there."

"Hey," LuAnn said, but she couldn't muster the indignation she wanted to. Her fingers were curled around a mug of tea, and the soft wisps of fragrant steam were calming. "I didn't cause the fire."

"No, but you do have a way of ending up wherever the excitement is," Janice said. She adjusted the throw pillow behind herself and leaned back against the couch cushions. The windows on the fourth floor were open to catch the cool breeze that had blown in that afternoon, and they could hear cicadas humming gently in the quiet evening.

LuAnn couldn't really deny it, as much as she wanted to. Tess said that Jay had propped a chair from the laundry room under the closet doorknob, which explained why she hadn't been able to open it. LuAnn then explained how she'd figured out for sure who Jay was and how she'd confronted him. How he'd confessed but then done everything he could to make sure his secret never got out.

"Your own uncle tried to kill you," Tess said. "That's terrible."

"I don't know what he thought would happen," LuAnn said. "Maybe he just wanted a chance to get away." She saw the look that passed between Janice and Tess, but she didn't know.

Had he really set that fire, hoping she'd perish in the flames? Or had he thought that the distraction would allow him time to get some distance, to think through what he'd done and what would happen now that LuAnn knew? She wanted to give him the benefit of the doubt—he was her flesh and blood, after all—even if all signs pointed to him not deserving it.

"The real question is, what are you going to do now?" Janice asked.

LuAnn had thought about that. She'd already decided she wasn't going to press charges. Jack would be in enough legal jeopardy for setting the fire in the hotel, not to mention for burning down the funeral home all those years ago and committing identity theft. As far as she knew there was no statute of limitations for arson. But she had also made another decision.

"I need to tell my cousins," she said. "They deserve to know their father is alive. I don't know how they will react, but they deserve to know the truth."

"We have his address," Janice reminded them.

Tess laughed. "We totally stalked him, remember? We know his address, his birth date, the value of his home, what he eats for breakfast..."

"We can't share that stuff, legally," LuAnn said. "But they all helped us get to the truth." She paused. "Thank you both for helping me get there."

"If you're thanking us for getting you trapped in that basement, forget it." Tess picked up a handful of popcorn from the bowl in front of her.

"No, not that. That was all my fault, I'm afraid." LuAnn took a sip of her tea, warm and comforting. "But for helping me dig until we found out who he really was. For not thinking I was crazy during this whole thing."

"We never said you weren't crazy," Tess said.

LuAnn smiled. It felt good to be here with her friends, as if everything was normal, after all that had happened. After what she'd discovered about Jay and about her own family history. She thought about her mother, believing for all those years that her youngest brother Jack was dead, when he'd really just run off and started a new life. LuAnn was almost glad Mom wasn't around to find out the truth. It would have broken her heart to know the depth of the deception that Jack had pulled off, how he'd chosen a new life and a new family over the people who mourned his death. Yes, it was probably good that her mother never found out about Jack.

But LuAnn hadn't ever felt closer to her since her passing than she did this week. That counted for something. LuAnn still didn't understand—would probably never understand— how Jack could do what he'd done. How he'd thought he could simply walk away from his family and act like they didn't exist. Family, home, the people and place that shape you—they are a part of you. They are in your blood. It's who you are.

But then, she thought, looking around at the friends she'd chosen to spend these years with, *sometimes family is more than blood. Sometimes family is people who love and support you, even when they think you're nuts. Sometimes family is the people who race toward a burning building to find you. Sometimes, family is the people you choose.* And LuAnn had never been more grateful she'd chosen to spend these days with her two best friends.

CHAPTER TWENTY-TWO

March 13, 1860

Prudence recognized him at once. He was older, thinner, frailer. The years had not been kind to her father—he had endured much, that was clear. But the moment he stepped down off the buggy into her yard, she saw it was him. The years could not erase his striking profile, the proud set of his shoulders, the dark hair, now threaded with gray. His face broke into a wide smile when he saw her.

Prudence wanted to run to him, but she hesitated, adjusting Moses in her arms. She had not seen her father since she was twelve years old. Would he even recognize her?

But she needn't have worried. As soon as his boots hit the ground, he let out a cry. It took her a moment to realize that he'd called out "Effie!"

Hearing her childhood name from her father's lips after all these years broke something inside of Prudence. Her composure left her, and she felt herself running. "Papa!"

She was in his arms, the strong, safe arms that had held her on so many dark nights, and tears were streaming down her cheeks. She could barely even see through the scrim of tears, but she didn't have to. He held her and rocked her, and she was bawling like a baby right there in the yard for all to see.

"You're grown up," he said, still holding her. Moses struggled between them.

"Yes, Papa." She didn't know what more to say. All those years, taken from them. All those years of not knowing if the other was alive or dead. All those years taken from them by the greed of a system that believed people could be bought, sold, and owned. It renewed her passion for ferrying those who escaped to safety just thinking about it. But for now, all she needed was this. To finally be with her father again.

"Now let me see this little fellow," Papa said, pulling back to take a look at Moses. He was nearing a year old now, and was already starting to resemble Papa, with his dark hair and dark eyes. Prudence held him out, but Papa didn't take the boy, just smiled as he studied him. "You've done well, Effie. You've—my goodness. Little Effie, all grown up. I can't believe it."

"It's so good to see thee again," she said, and then cringed. Her people didn't speak that way. She'd picked up the Quaker way of speaking, but her family had never been so formal. She'd need to remember to drop the thees and thous around him. "I still can't believe I found you after all this time."

"I can't either. Oh, but Effie, I am so, so glad you did."

He pulled her in for another hug, and Prudence let herself relax in his arms. She had so many questions—where had he been all this time? What had happened to him after she escaped? How had he survived? When had he escaped? Did he know who else from their community was still around?

But the questions would wait. For now, she was in her father's arms, and that was something she'd never expected to happen again. It was as if he'd come back from the dead. For now, she would simply enjoy knowing that he was alive, and he was here. Her family might be broken and scattered, but her father was alive, and he had come back to her. That was all she wanted to think about for now.

CHAPTER TWENTY-THREE

Sunlight filtered through the leaves of the live oak trees, dappling the yard and the tables with a gorgeous golden glow. Oldies music poured through the speakers they'd set up around the lawn, and Lauren and Ethan—now officially Mr. and Mrs. Hansen—were twirling on the makeshift dance floor, the hem of Lauren's hot-pink knee-length wedding dress spinning out around her.

The ceremony, they'd been told, had gone off without a hitch, and by the time the guests started arriving at the reception, they were set up and ready. It truly had turned out beautifully.

After the week they'd had, it was no small miracle that they'd managed to pull it off. LuAnn was still haunted by the cold fear of being locked in that basement, and the police chase that had culminated in Jay's arrest outside the hotel he'd just checked into in Pennsylvania was as dramatic as it was disturbing. Jacqueline had been shocked, of course, and though it was far too early to know what would happen, she'd indicated that she hoped they would be able to work through this. LuAnn would pray for them. Even a strong marriage would struggle under the weight of the revelations that had come out about

Jay's past. Marriage, she thought, watching the newlyweds swaying under the trees in front of her, was worth fighting for.

They'd hired Taylor and Robin to walk around passing out the appetizers, and the food was going over well. The mac and cheese bites seemed to be a particular hit. Soon they would set out the food for the buffet, and then the spectacular three-tiered cake, dripping with flowers and lacy icing, that sat in the walk-in refrigerator downstairs.

LuAnn had called Denise yesterday and told her the news. To say Denise had been shocked was an understatement. But she'd promised to call her brothers and to think about what this meant for them. She thought she probably wanted to meet Jay eventually. It would take some time, but LuAnn thought she would probably get there. She would pray for that as well.

LuAnn was just setting the huge dish of Winnie's special sirloin tips into the warming tray when Brad walked up beside her.

LuAnn tensed, remembering their last exchange.

"Hi there," he said, ducking his head a bit. Even though she wasn't sure what to expect from this interaction—had even dreaded it, in fact—she had to admit that he looked very nice in a dark suit and light-blue tie that brought out the color of his eyes.

"Hi."

"This is truly beautiful. You all did a fabulous job." He clutched a glass of iced tea in his hand.

LuAnn looked around again. He was right. Couples were dancing, and groups of friends were chatting, and there was a line at the photo booth. The long tables draped in white linens looked gorgeous under the trees, and the punches of color from the flowers were just perfect. Beyond it all, the sun was starting to set over the river, and LuAnn knew that soon the fairy lights would twinkle on, and the scene would become even more breathtaking. Most importantly, though, Lauren seemed to be loving it. Apparently, she truly was the most laid-back bride in history, and genuinely seemed simply happy to be married to the love of her life. Nothing else seemed to matter to her. There was something almost magical about that, LuAnn thought. She wondered how many marriages these days might be different if more weddings were focused on the marriage instead of what would look good in pictures. Then again, LuAnn had never actually been married, so maybe she couldn't say.

"Thank you." Brad's words brought her back to the present.

"Of course."

"No, I mean, thank you for all of this"—he gestured around at the party spread out before them—"but also, thank you for being brave enough to say what you said."

LuAnn looked up tentatively.

"You were right, of course."

"What do you mean?"

"I mean, I refused to see it, but you were right. My hesitation about Ethan really didn't have anything to do with Ethan. It had more to do with the idea of Lauren growing up."

A hundred thoughts rushed through her mind. She had been right. She'd been right, and he admitted it.

"She's always been special to you," LuAnn said. "It makes sense."

"She always has been special," Brad said. "But, as you pointed out, it's not like we don't have any nieces. Saffron is my niece, and I don't feel quite as protective about her, so I started to think about why that might be. And I realized that, in some ways, it meant something that Mark chose us."

"That makes sense." It did. Family was everything, but the family you chose was in some ways even more special.

"But it's not just that. Stephanie and I thought of Lauren as the daughter we never had. When she was a little girl, she was so much a part of our lives. And...I don't know. I guess with Lauren growing up, getting married...It just feels like the last link to that time is gone."

LuAnn reached out and gently placed her hand on Brad's arm. He let a soft smile curve his lips, but he didn't say anything.

His last link to Stephanie was what he meant. Lauren getting married was bringing up the pain of losing his wife, and that's what caused his animosity toward Ethan. LuAnn tried not to let that thought pierce her.

Of course he missed his wife. He always would. You didn't just get over losing someone who was your whole world. Somehow she knew this, in the same way she knew that the pain of her mother's passing would get better over the years, but it would never go away. There would always be a hole where her presence had been. LuAnn had her scrapbooks and her diaries and her memories, and Brad had...Well, Brad had those things, but he also had Lauren. But now Lauren was moving on, and that made him miss his wife even more.

"It makes sense," she said again. "And it's understandable. Of course you miss her."

"It's not—" He paused, struggling for words. "It's not that, really." Then he turned and took LuAnn's hand. He took a deep breath. "I guess what I'm trying to say is, yes, seeing all this has brought up memories, both of the good times and the times we really struggled. All those years we wanted a child, and our prayers were always met with a 'no.'" His voice trailed off for a moment, and then he shook his head. "But I guess what I'm trying to say is, with this wedding, I've realized that it's finally time to stop hanging on to all that. It's time to start thinking about the future, instead of hanging on to the past."

As they stood there on the patio, watching Lauren and her new husband dance under the trees, Brad threaded his fingers through LuAnn's. LuAnn's breath caught, and she held it for a moment, thinking. Did he mean...But he didn't say anything more. They just stood there together, watching the party around them.

Maybe he did mean that he could see them as more than friends. Maybe someday. LuAnn had been so insistent for all this time that they were just friends, but the way her heart leapt at his words, she wondered if she was being totally honest with herself. Could there be more than friendship in their future?

LuAnn didn't know what to think. But for now, she had a wedding to host, and she reluctantly pulled herself away.

"As much as I want to stay, I'm afraid I have to get back to getting dinner on the table," she said.

"I know," he said, letting her pull her fingers away. "But before the evening is out, you owe me a dance." He gestured to the dance floor, where Lauren and Ethan were currently doing some strange form of the twist.

"It's a deal," she said, and gave him one last long smile before she turned and headed inside.

If the Lord had it in His plans, there would be many more long nights on patios and dancing under the trees in their future. For now, she was grateful for the chance to be here, at this beautiful inn, and enjoy nights like this. For now, she would simply take every day as a gift and do her best to enjoy every moment.

Dear Reader,

Like most books I write, this one started with an idea…
I wonder what would happen if…. I'd hear rumors (no doubt totally
false) about people who supposedly walked away from the twin
towers of 9/11 and started a new life, and that got me wondering
if a mystery could be created out of a similarly devastating event.

The Farmington Mine Disaster is sadly, terribly real. Ninety-
nine miners were inside the mine when the explosion happened,
and only twenty-one of them made it out. Nineteen of the bodies
were never recovered. Haunting photos of the aftermath show
towering plumes of smoke looming over the entire small town,
which of course was devastated by the loss of so many men.
Though the cause of the explosion was never determined for
certain, there is some evidence that a safety alarm—which
would have given the men inside a signal to evacuate—had
been disabled. The disaster was the impetus for new safety
legislation in the United States.

I have to confess that I have never visited West Virginia,
but my grandparents are both from Parkersburg, and my
mom—though she was a navy brat and moved around a
lot—considers the state home. It was fun to get to know her
home state a bit better, and I talked with her and my aunt about
what a regional accent would sound like and what it was like to
live there in the 1960s. All errors are, naturally, my own.

I hope you enjoy *Stolen Goodbyes* as much as I enjoyed
writing it!

Best wishes,
Beth Adams

ABOUT THE AUTHOR

Beth Adams lives in Brooklyn, New York, with her husband and two young daughters. When she's not writing, she spends her time cleaning up after two devious cats and trying to find time to read mysteries.

THE OHIO RIVER MUSEUM

The Ohio River Museum's gift shop is the site of a wallet theft in this story, but the museum is so much more than just a gift shop. The museum is dedicated to preserving and celebrating the important role the Ohio River played in our nation's westward expansion. The exhibits showcase the history of the riverboats that plied its waters, carrying cargo and passengers, including the infamous sternwheelers that live so large in our collective memory. There is information about locks and dams, boat construction before the era of power tools, and boat whistles and bells. There's also a restored shanty boat—an early houseboat of sorts—as well as a series of poles marking the high-water marks of the worst floods in the town's history. There's even a historic sternwheeler, the W.P. Snyder Jr., that you can tour. The museum gives a fascinating look at life in this historic river town, and is well worth a visit.

Something Delicious from our Wayfarers Inn Friends

Janice's Fresh Tomato Sauce

One of my favorite easy summer dinners is pasta with fresh tomato sauce, like Janice makes in this story. It's ridiculously easy to make, and tastes so much better than the kind you buy in a jar. You can even use canned tomatoes when tomatoes aren't in season, but if you can find good-quality heirloom tomatoes in summer, use those here. Some purists would insist that you peel your tomatoes before you use them in a sauce, but I never do.

¼ cup extra virgin olive oil

3–4 garlic cloves, crushed

2 28-oz cans whole or diced plum tomatoes, or 3–4 pounds fresh

10–15 leaves fresh basil, slivered

salt and pepper to taste

1–2 tablespoons butter, optional

Heat olive oil in large skillet over medium heat. Add garlic and cook until it smells toasty, but doesn't brown. Add tomatoes, salt, and pepper. Bring to a simmer and cook until sauce has thickened and tomatoes have mostly fallen apart. This will probably take 30–40 minutes. Stop cooking when sauce reaches the consistency you prefer. Add basil. Taste and adjust seasoning. If you're feeling really decadent, slip in a tablespoon or two of good-quality butter and stir until it melts. You won't regret it, even if your doctor disagrees—it adds a richness and depth to the sauce. Serve over freshly-cooked pasta.

Read on for a sneak peek of another exciting book
in the Secrets of Wayfarers Inn series!

RED, WHITE, AND TRUE
by Leslie Gould

Tess Wallace stepped behind the front desk in the lobby of Wayfarers Inn, pushing her hair away from her sweaty forehead. She'd been running up and down the stairs all evening, trying to accommodate the Hines family.

It would have been nice if the entire family had gone down to the river to watch the Fourth of July fireworks, but the older adults and younger children had stayed behind. Most were on the back patio, enjoying time together playing board games under the stringed lights that criss-crossed the space, but Granny Hines had insisted on staying in her room. Elijah, her teenage grandson, had stayed in his too.

Tess sank onto the stool behind the desk, glad to give her aching feet a rest. She glanced appreciatively around the lobby at the red, white, and blue bunting that Janice had strung throughout the bottom floor of the inn, including the café. Tess was what Janice called "decoratively challenged." So she stuck to what she did best—finances and hospitality—while LuAnn, the third member of their Inn Crowd, kept them organized and up to code.

Tess's eyes lit on the curio cabinet that stood against a wall several feet away, and she groaned. She rose to her feet and, for what seemed the umpteenth time in two days, tried once more to get the bunting to stay attached to the top of the cabinet. The cabinet was a new addition to the lobby and housed an exhibit from the Marietta Underground Railroad Museum. It held a first edition of *Uncle Tom's Cabin* and a few other things— including a pamphlet, a shawl, an old pair of boots, and a knife.

As Tess collapsed onto the stool again, the phone rang. She glanced at the caller ID and groaned. Elijah. Then she smiled before she answered it, hoping it would cheer up her voice, which otherwise would sound as exhausted as she felt. "This is Tess. How may I help you?"

"I need to speak with your IT department."

She sighed. Yes, it was Elijah. "I already told you," she said. "We don't have an IT department." He'd been complaining all evening about how slow the Wi-Fi was.

"You have to have someone who handles your technology." He obviously wasn't even trying to hide the exasperation in his voice.

"I'm not sure what else to tell you…" Tess raised her head to see Elijah's mother, Val, standing in front of her, reaching for the phone. Her husband was Granny Hines's son, but he wasn't able to come on the trip. Tess gathered, from what Val said, that he owned a start-up business that was struggling. However, Val seemed absolutely devoted to her mother-in-law and spent more time taking care of Granny than Granny's own daughters.

"I'll talk to him," Val said with a stern look on her thin face. Tess handed the receiver to her.

Val pressed the receiver to her ear, tugged on a heart necklace around her neck with her free hand, and said slowly, "Elijah, leave Tess alone. She's been running around all evening trying to accommodate you. You're here to spend time with family—not play computer games."

Tess couldn't hear what the boy said back.

"We'll talk when I come upstairs. In the meantime, don't call Tess again. If you do, you'll need to come out on the patio with the rest of us." Val said goodbye and then handed the phone back to Tess. "I'm so sorry."

"It's not a problem," Tess said. She liked Val. She was no-nonsense. Not nearly as intense as her daughter Keeley, who was interning with Maybelline Rector, the curator at the Marietta Underground Railroad Museum. Keeley had put together the exhibit in the curio cabinet and had visited the inn many times to double-check something or to test the alarm. For a while it seemed as if she were on staff at Wayfarers and not the museum. The young woman, who was a junior in college and majoring in history, was the sole reason her family had chosen Marietta—and the inn—for their family reunion. She was in Marietta for the summer, renting a room with a local family. The extended Hines family had rented every room except for one. Keeley was great to have around, but she definitely took her position at the museum seriously.

Val ran her hand through her short dark hair. "Between Granny and Elijah, we're quite a handful."

Tess hastened to reassure her. "We do what we can to accommodate our guests, although I'm not sure there's anything we can do about the Wi-Fi." No one had ever complained about it being slow before.

"Nor should you," Val said. "In fact, please don't. Maybe it will get him off his laptop. I didn't even know he'd brought it along until we got here. He hates to travel and wanted to stay home alone, but I forced him to come." The boy was probably sixteen or so and was sharing Woodsmoke and Pine with his cousins, Chad and Chet, eight-year-old twins who made Tess's four-year-old triplet grandchildren seem like the calmest children in the world.

Tess could understand not wanting to leave Elijah home alone. The Hineses lived in California, a San Francisco suburb, if she remembered the address correctly. It wasn't as if they lived in a small, sleepy town.

She pushed her hair away from her forehead again. Had it gotten warmer?

Val glanced toward the patio door. "I think it might be cooler outside than inside now."

"Oh, dear." Tess stood. "So it's not just me?"

Val shook her head. "It's definitely warm in here."

Tess stepped out from behind the desk and placed her hand against the register in the wall. The forced air certainly wasn't cool. In fact, it felt downright warm. She turned the corner to the thermostat. Goodness, the temperature was up to seventy-nine. Warm air was worse than no air. She turned the system off and tried to think of a diversion for her guests.

"Winnie made a delicious red, white, and blue tart today. There's a pan left. Could your group take it off our hands?" Winnie's tarts had never failed them yet.

"Oh, that sounds wonderful," Val answered. "Can I help?"

"Sure. Follow me." Tess led the way into the kitchen and handed Val a stack of plates and a handful of forks and napkins. She retrieved the tarts from the refrigerator, and the two women headed out to the patio just as the first of the fireworks exploded over the river with a terrific boom. Tess jumped, and the whole building seemed to shake. The group squealed in delight. Sparkler-like stars in red, white, and blue filled the dark sky.

Val pointed to the tarts before another firework exploded. "Look, guys!"

Everyone oohed and aahed as Tess set the blueberry and raspberry tarts, dusted with powdered sugar, on the table. The group included Granny's daughters, Connie and Ellen, their husbands, Bob and Gary, and Chad and Chet, who were Connie and Bob's sons. Sadie and Collette, Ellen and Gary's teenage daughters, were off with Keeley and watching the display over the river. As another firework exploded, they all turned their attention back to the sky, and Tess quietly slipped back into the inn.

As she headed down the stairs to the basement, several more booms shook the building. She'd always loved the Fourth of July, and the town of Marietta did an exceptional job celebrating it.

Today wasn't turning out to be Tess's favorite Fourth though. She'd felt unsettled all day. She'd opened a financial investment statement that morning for an account managed by a man who'd been a friend of her late husband's. The man, Frank Bryant, owned an investment company that Jeffrey had invested in a decade ago. Tess had been ready to cash it out after Jeffrey died, but Frank assured her he'd keep earning her money. Now the account had taken a big dive.

She'd been trying not to worry about it, at least not until she could call Frank in the morning, but the situation kept nagging at her, so much so that she'd told Janice and LuAnn to go ahead and go watch the fireworks. She didn't mind seeing to their guests in the inn.

Last Fourth of July, LuAnn, Janice, and Tess had recently purchased Wayfarers Inn and were knee-deep in renovations. The three of them had been eager to finish and open the inn. Now, after ten months of being in business, most of the kinks of running the inn had been worked out. She couldn't imagine that anything serious could be wrong with the AC system. It was brand new.

She stood in front of it in the furnace room of the basement, on the opposite end of the underground tunnel that had truly put Wayfarers Inn on the map. Of course, the inn had been heated by coal during the 1800s. Now the furnace was natural gas, and the forced air was electric. She tried to remember the last time the filters had been changed. Thorn would know, but she wouldn't ask him to come over this late. Another boom caught Tess off guard. It sounded like a cannon. The river would be packed with residents and tourists, their heads turned toward the bursts of red, white, and blue against the dark sky, celebrating the USA growing another year older. It truly was a wonderful day—even if she felt out of sorts.

She sighed as she stared at the air conditioning unit. She pulled out a filter, but it didn't seem to be dirty. It was probably some electronic problem. Maybe it just needed to be reprogrammed. Not knowing what else to do, she sent an SOS text to LuAnn and Janice. An inn with no AC in July was an emergency. Eighty-nine and muggy was the high for the day. Tomorrow, it was supposed to be over ninety. She opened her phone app to call Thorn for advice, but another boom caught her off guard. She jumped again and then laughed at herself—until the crash of glass, followed by the sound of an alarm she didn't recognize, truly frightened her.

Tess bounded up the stairs, wondering what else could have possibly gone wrong. She stopped at the top of the stairs, ready to head to the kitchen. But as she hurried into the lobby, she saw that the curio cabinet had been broken into. The alarm continued to wail.

Tess stepped closer. Shards of glass covered the floor, while jagged pieces still hung in the cabinet. Tess had no idea how to turn the alarm off. She needed Maybelline. Or Keeley. ASAP.

A Note from the Editors

We hope you enjoy Secrets of Wayfarers Inn, created by the Books and Inspirational Media Division of Guideposts, a nonprofit organization that touches millions of lives every day through products and services that inspire, encourage, help you grow in your faith, and celebrate God's love in every aspect of your daily life.

Thank you for making a difference with your purchase of this book, which helps fund our many outreach programs to military personnel, prisons, hospitals, nursing homes, and educational institutions. To learn more, visit Guideposts Foundation.org.

We also maintain many useful and uplifting online resources. Visit Guideposts.org to read true stories of hope and inspiration, access OurPrayer network, sign up for free newsletters, download free e-books, join our Facebook community, and follow our stimulating blogs.

To learn about other Guideposts publications, including the best-selling devotional *Daily Guideposts*, go to ShopGuideposts .org, call (800) 932-2145, or write to Guideposts, PO Box 5815, Harlan, Iowa 51593.

Sign up for the
Guideposts Fiction Newsletter
and stay up-to-date on
the books you love!

guideposts·fiction

Inspiring reads chosen just for you!

What's New

Mysteries of Martha's Vineyard

Come to the shores of this quaint and historic island and dig in to a cozy mystery. When a recent widow inherits a lighthouse just off the coast of Massachusetts, she finds exciting adventures, new friends, and renewed hope.

On the quaint and historic island of Martha's Vineyard, just off the coast of Massachusetts, Priscilla comes face-to-face with adventure—one that includes rediscovered family, new friends, old homes, and head-scratching mysteries that crop up with surprising regularity. Learn More

Reader Favorite

Tearoom Mysteries

Take a quaint New England town... add some hidden treasures... a few suspicious characters... and a good measure of faith and friendship and you've brewed up Tearoom Mysteries!

Come explore this quaint village with its picturesque mountain lake surrounded by wild blueberry bushes, at your leisure. Like the people who come to Elaine and Jan's tearoom, you'll find yourself feeling relaxed. Learn More

From Our Editors

Sugarcreek Amish Mysteries

Sit back and enjoy a vacation for your soul with Sugarcreek Amish Mysteries. These well-written stories of the strong bond that develops between two women of vastly different backgrounds and traditions will tug at your heartstrings and provide hours of entertainment, intrigue, and wonder. In addition to Cheryl's keen insight and excellent riddle solving ability, you'll love experiencing Naomi's proverbial Amish wisdom and exploring her down-to-earth faith. Learn More

A perfect blend of faith, family, and fun!

You'll get sneak peeks of new releases, recommendations from other Guideposts readers, and special offers just for you . . .
and it's FREE!

Just go to Guideposts.org/Newsletters
today to sign up.

Guideposts.

**Visit Guideposts.org/Shop
or call (800) 932-2145**